Battling in the Pacific

Soldiering in World War II

Alaska
(USA)

OCEAN

Oahu

HAWAIIAN
ISLANDS

Japanese
attack on
Pearl Harbor

Wake
Island

MARSHALL
ISLANDS

GILBERT
ISLANDS

Battle of
Tarawa

SOLDIERS ON THE BATTLEFRONT

BATTLING IN THE PACIFIC

SOLDIERING IN WORLD WAR II

Susan Provost Beller

Twenty-First Century Books · Minneapolis

To Jim, the second of my "in-law kids"

Title page image: A lone U.S. Marine looks out at the results of the bombardment of Okinawa, Japan, in 1945.

Text copyright © 2008 by Susan Provost Beller

Twenty-First Century Books
A division of Lerner Publishing Group, Inc.
241 First Avenue North
Minneapolis, Minnesota 55401 U.S.A.

Website address: www.lernerbooks.com

Library of Congress Cataloging-in-Publication Data

Beller, Susan Provost, 1949–
    Battling in the Pacific : soldiering in World War II / by Susan Provost Beller.
       p.   cm. — (Soldiers on the battlefront)
    Includes bibliographical references and index.
    ISBN-13: 978–0–8225–6381–5 (lib. bdg. : alk. paper)
    ISBN-10: 0–8225–6381–9 (lib. bdg. : alk. paper)
    1. World War, 1939–1945— Campaigns—Pacific Area—Juvenile literature. 2. United States—Armed Forces—History—World War, 1939–1945—Juvenile literature. I. Title.
D767.B44 2008
940.54'26—dc22   2006028168

Manufactured in the United States of America
1 2 3 4 5 6 — JR — 13 12 11 10 09 08

Contents

> **"The United States was suddenly and deliberately attacked by naval and air forces of the Empire of Japan."**
>
> —Franklin Delano Roosevelt, 1941

PROLOGUE

Sitting in Pearl Harbor on the Hawaiian island of Oahu are two warships. They represent the story of U.S. participation in World War II in the Pacific (1941–1945). One of them—the USS *Arizona*—lies at the bottom of the harbor. It was destroyed on December 7, 1941, in the surprise Japanese attack that led the United States into the war. The other is the USS *Missouri*. This powerful battleship joined the ensuing war and became the site of the Japanese surrender on September 2, 1945.

Most visitors who go to Pearl Harbor stand on the USS *Arizona* National Memorial. The ship is visible just below the surface of the water. Visitors can see the oil bubbles still slowly leaking to the surface. The 1,177 men who lost their lives during the Japanese attack remain entombed below.

Near the *Arizona*'s resting site looms the *Missouri*. It is a huge battleship, whose size alone catches visitors' attention. The ship's guns can throw an explosive artillery shell the size of a car to a target 20 miles away. Mighty Mo, as the USS *Missouri* is

Dedicated in 1962, the USS *Arizona* National Memorial at Pearl Harbor spans the midsection of the ship's sunken hull. The memorial honors the 1,177 men who lost their lives when Japanese bombers sank the *Arizona* on December 7, 1941.

affectionately known, still looks ready to go into battle.

It is entirely fitting that the *Missouri* retired so close to the *Arizona.* Between the two ships lies a distance of less than 0.5 mile. Within this short distance, soldiers witnessed the beginning and end of U.S. participation in the largest war the world has ever known. Four years of bitter fighting ended with 292,000 American deaths in battle. The two ships are the "bookends" that bracket U.S. involvement in World War II in the Pacific theater of operations (area of fighting).

The USS *Missouri* steams toward its final docking place at Pearl Harbor in 1998. The U.S. government allowed the *Missouri* to become a museum. Japanese leaders had signed the surrender documents that ended World War II on the ship.

A COMPLEX WAR

World War I (1914–1918) was called the war to end all wars. But then came World War II (1939–1945), which, in many ways, was a continuation of that war. The peace agreement signed after World War I placed the blame squarely on defeated Germany. Harsh penalties were forced upon that country.

Germany suffered a legacy of anger and humiliation. The country also experienced harsh economic conditions. Then the entire world endured an economic depression in the late 1920s and into the 1930s. These hardships fueled even more unrest in Germany.

Dictatorships arose in three countries—Germany, Italy, and Japan. These dictatorships had strong militaries. The governments controlled the lives of the people. Each of these countries supported a policy of what Adolf Hitler, the German leader, called *Lebensraum*, or living space. At a conference in 1937, Hitler argued that the German people needed living space. He said they were justified in taking land from surrounding countries because of the natural superiority of the Germans.

The German and Japanese governments both believed that their people were racially superior to those in other countries. They argued that their needs justified any action necessary to expand their territory. These countries began to put their ideas into action. In September 1939, Germany invaded Poland in eastern Europe. Britain and France started to fight back, and the war in Europe began. Within a year, Hitler's forces had overrun most of the continent. Japan joined an alliance with Germany and Italy in 1940. Meanwhile, Japanese forces had taken control of much of Southeast Asia and parts of China.

For the United States, it was a time to watch and wait. The 1941 attack on Pearl Harbor ended the wait and brought the United States into the conflict. Fighting for the Americans began in the Pacific and ended in the Pacific. But U.S. troops also fought this war in Europe, in North Africa, and in other locations in Asia. They fought on land, in the air, and on the sea.

In modern times, this complex war seems simpler. Yet it remains the story of how troops define honor. The story also includes an enemy whose ideas about honor in war perplexed the Americans who faced them in battle. The two ships, these "bookends" of war, stand for a conflict that touched the world.

> "As the strafer [firing airplane] banked, I noticed the…insignia on his wing tips. Until then I…had not known who attacked us."
>
> —Pharmacist's Mate Lee Soucy, on the USS *Utah*, 1941

CHAPTER ONE

THE DAY OF INFAMY

The European part of World War II began in 1939 with the invasion of Poland. In response, Britain, France, and their allies (collectively known as the Allies) declared war on Germany. Opposing the Allies were the Axis powers, which by 1940 included Germany, Italy, and Japan. After invading Poland, Hitler's troops quickly conquered Denmark, Norway, Luxembourg, Belgium, and France. Then they began an air attack on Britain. In spite of the devastation Germany was causing, Americans remained divided over how the country should respond to the German threat. Although many Americans sided with the Allies, they were still not ready to join the fight. They were content to remain neutral.

President Franklin Delano Roosevelt did not agree. He and many other Americans believed that if Hitler was not stopped in Europe, he would eventually become a direct threat to the United States. Roosevelt pursued all possible ways to aid the Allies without actually declaring war.

U.S. law required that, as a neutral country, the United States could not give war materials to countries actively participating in the war. Congress approved cash sales only. However, after the fall of France, Britain began to use up its supply of money for buying arms and equipment.

President Roosevelt then came up with the Lend-Lease Act. It allowed the United States to lend war materials to the Allies. But this was as far as the country could go in supporting the Allies without entering the war. Meanwhile, however, the United States encouraged its industries to switch from making goods to making war materials. U.S. soldiers would need these materials if the country entered the war.

World War II started in Europe. German soldiers from the Nazi army goose step (march) through Poland, which Germany invaded in 1939.

CONFLICT WITH JAPAN

At this time, a group of military leaders led by General Hideki Tojo ruled Japan. The Tojo regime saw continual expansion and control of surrounding land as crucial to the island nation's economic growth. As a result, Japan and the United States were coming into increasing conflict over control of the Pacific Ocean. Japanese leaders believed that Japan's national security depended on expanding control farther into the ocean. This would mean moving into U.S-controlled territories, such as the Philippines.

By 1941 leaders in both nations believed that a U.S-Japanese war was inevitable. But such a war was daunting to Japan. The United States was a huge and powerful country. It had seemingly unlimited resources and great manufacturing power. Japanese military leaders believed that the only way to defeat the United States would be to cripple its navy in one massive surprise attack. Then, with its navy in ruins, the United States would have no way of stopping Japanese expansion in the Pacific.

Japanese admiral Isoroku Yamamoto developed a bold and risky plan of attack. It was so risky that most U.S. military experts of

Hideki Tojo held many positions in the Japanese government before becoming prime minister in 1941. After the war, he was hanged as a war criminal.

Isoroku Yamamoto planned the surprise attack on Pearl Harbor. Japanese planes took off from several aircraft carriers to reach the faraway island of Oahu in the U.S. territory of Hawaii.

the time probably would have rejected it as impossible. In fact, the United States would need to be caught off guard for it to work. But the Americans had a weapon unknown to the Japanese. They had cracked the code the Japanese used in their confidential messages to their diplomats and military leaders.

Communication is important when trying to manage military actions. So having access to Japanese signals gave the United States a huge advantage. The U.S. government felt confident that it could anticipate any moves made by the Japanese. U.S. leaders were not worried about the Japanese launching a surprise attack.

In addition, U.S. military leaders assumed that a Japanese attack on the U.S. territory of Hawaii would be impossible. No country could attack the United States from 6,000 miles away. Instead, they were on alert for a Japanese attack on U.S. bases in the Philippines or other areas closer to Japan.

Admiral Yamamoto was far more daring than expected. His plans were to be carried out without any communications among the naval forces under his command. This combination proved to be a deadly shock to the Americans.

Soldiers and sailors stare in shock at the fire and destruction at Pearl Harbor.

First Minutes

It was a quiet Sunday morning on December 7, 1941, at Pearl Harbor on the Hawaiian island of Oahu. Many of the sailors and marines stationed at the base were on board the USS *Arizona* and seven other ships grouped together on what was called Battleship Row. The men were carrying out their normal routines. A number of the ships' officers were spending the weekend on the base because they didn't have to be on board at all times. No one knew that Japanese planes were on their way, having already taken off from six aircraft carriers.

Shortly before eight in the morning, Japanese pilots broke radio silence to give the signal to attack. Hundreds of Japanese aircraft suddenly filled the sky over the harbor. A wave of fighter planes—small, fast, and agile aircraft—attacked the U.S. airfields on Oahu.

Their mission was to destroy the U.S. planes on the ground before they could respond. Within minutes, the low-flying planes, with their machine guns blasting nonstop, wiped out most of the U.S. fighters.

Soon Japanese dive-bombers were all over the harbor. They unloaded bombs and torpedoes (self-propelled bombs that strike ships below the waterline) on the fleet along Battleship Row. U.S. sailors and marines scrambled to their battle stations. But for many, even in the first moments of the attack, it was already too late.

On the USS *Oklahoma*, Seaman Stephen Young heard the jarring alarm known as general quarters. He hurried to his battle station. At first he was annoyed that his superior officers would call for a drill on a Sunday morning. Then "he felt the ship quiver" and "a heave of the deck." This was no drill.

Men escape the capsized and sinking USS *Oklahoma (left)*, which took direct hits during the Japanese attack. The USS *Maryland (right)* was not as damaged. It later sailed to a shipyard in Washington State to be repaired.

Moments after the attack began, Japanese aircraft struck the USS *Arizona* with bombs and torpedoes. The ship exploded and sank, trapping 1,177 men inside. One historian wrote: "Hundreds of men were cut down in a single, searing flash. . . . One fire control man simply vanished—the only place he could have gone was through the narrow range-finder slot. . . . Over 1000 men were gone."

Marine private James Cory was on the *Arizona* that morning and was one of the lucky men who survived. Yet he was left with horrible memories of the "zombies" walking the deck "burned completely white . . . hair was burned off; their eyebrows were burned off." There were, he remembered, "steel fragments in the air, fire, oil . . . pieces of boat deck, canvas . . . lots of steel and bodies

Flames and smoke engulf several ships on Battleship Row, as small boats try to rescue survivors.

coming down . . . a thigh and a leg; I saw fingers; I saw hands; I saw elbows and arms."

Aviation machinist D. A. Graham, also on the *Arizona*, saw "lots of men coming out on the quarterdeck [upper deck] with every stitch of clothing and shoes blown off, painfully burned and shocked." Historians' best guess is that the *Arizona* took hits from eight bombs and a number of torpedoes. The ship and the men on board who were killed became symbols of the horror of the attack.

> **"Hundreds of men were cut down in a single, searing flash. . . . One fire control man simply vanished. . . ."**
>
> —James Cory, 1941

THE BATTLESHIPS

By the time a second wave of Japanese bombers had finished attacking, three battleships—the USS *Arizona*, the USS *Utah*, and the USS *Oklahoma*—were permanently damaged. Nearby, aboard the cruiser USS *Raleigh*, Captain R. Bentham Simons watched in horror as the *Utah* sank. He was unable to help the crew trying to escape its fate. The ship "was turning over very rapidly," he remembered. "The heavy beams," used in support of its guns, "were rolling down on the unfortunate members of the crew."

Pharmacist's Mate Lee Soucy was on the *Utah* as it went down and described his frantic efforts to get away. "The bugler sounded 'General Quarters,'" he wrote. As Soucy was trying to get to his battle station, a second torpedo hit and "the ship was already listing [leaning to one side]." Told to abandon ship, he found the water no safer, as the Japanese gunners strafed (fired at from an aircraft) the men trying to escape. "As the strafer banked," he remembered, "I

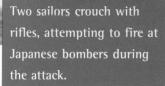

Two sailors crouch with rifles, attempting to fire at Japanese bombers during the attack.

noticed the big red insignia on his wing tips. [Japanese aircraft had a red circle on the top and bottom of each wing.] Until then I really had not known who attacked us."

For the Japanese, wiping out the U.S. ships was thrilling. Commander Midori Matsumura recalled his second pass through Battleship Row. One of his torpedoes struck the USS *West Virginia*. "A huge waterspout splashed over the stack of the ship and then tumbled down like an exhausted geyser. . . . What a magnificent sight."

REGROUPING

Amid the killings, the Americans began to fight back. The marines and sailors regrouped, despite the chaos and often even without orders from their leaders. Stories abound of groups of two or three men working antiaircraft guns that normally needed crews of fifteen. A sailor on the USS *Arizona* noted that "there was no going to pieces or growing panicky noticeable." In fact, in spite of everything, "The Stars and Stripes still flew from *Arizona*'s blackened, tilting superstructure."

Other accounts tell of guns on the *Arizona* still being used even as the ship lay wrecked in the water. One man repeatedly adjusted a gun barrel with his hands, unaware of the heat of the barrel and his hands blistering with burns. One sailor on the USS *Tennessee* "chopped a ten-inch hawser [rope] in half with one stroke." The men reacted with heroic deeds as if they were everyday actions. Aviation chief ordnanceman John Finn earned the Congressional Medal of Honor when he used a machine gun to return fire throughout the attack. He did this in spite of being wounded several times.

Explosions to the deck and hull doomed the USS *Arizona (right)*. Also taking hits on Battleship Row were the nearby USS *Tennessee (center)* and the USS *West Virginia (left)*. Both the *West Virginia* and the *Tennessee* were repaired. They eventually went back into service in the Pacific theater (area of fighting).

Others went out of their way to help the wounded. Rather than escaping to safety, Signalman Second Class Richard Burge stayed on the *Tennessee* and "helped remove wounded and dead from turret #2 [the small, cramped area where the crew who worked gun #2 were stationed]." He remembered "one sailor trying to talk. His flesh was falling off his face." The Japanese pilots continued to fire at the

WHAT HAPPENS WHEN THE SHIPS AREN'T NEEDED ANYMORE?

Did you ever wonder what becomes of the thousands and thousands of ships (or aircraft, tanks, and other equipment) that were built in wartime when the war ends? Some of them remain in service. Others are placed in museums.

The USS *Missouri*, for example, stopped being used in 1955. Then it was reactivated and saw service in the Persian Gulf War in 1991. After that it was removed from service once again and turned into a museum at Pearl Harbor.

Most of the fleet that served in the Pacific was decommissioned. That means the ship was removed from the active list of naval vessels and put in storage. Storing a ship is referred to as putting it in mothballs (even though most people don't even use mothballs anymore). Ships that are decommissioned can be kept available in case they are needed for future wars, which is what happened with the *Missouri*.

Decommissioning a ship is done with a ceremony that recognizes the ship's history and service. For U.S. naval ships, the ceremony begins with the raising of the flag, a prayer, and a set of rituals in which final reports are given from the officers of the ship. People who served on the ship in the past usually attend the ceremony. After all the guests and crew go ashore, the flag is lowered, and the ship is no longer part of the U.S. Navy.

If the ship is put in mothballs, it will eventually become too old to be used again. When it has no more useful life, the ship is sent to be broken apart and used for scrap metal.

wounded soldiers, which only added to the horror. Burge himself was forced to crawl beneath the anchor chain on the ship to try to get away from the "machine gun bullets... knocking sparks off the chain just inches from me. I thought my time had come."

The attack lasted less than two hours. But in that short time, the Japanese had crippled the U.S. fleet. More than 2,300 sailors and marines had been killed. Some 2,000 others had been wounded. The Japanese attack had destroyed or damaged 21 U.S. ships and more than 300 aircraft. The Japanese had lost 29 aircraft.

The following day, President Roosevelt spoke to Congress. His famous speech was broadcast on the radio to the American people. "Yesterday," he began, "December 7, 1941—a date which will live in infamy—the United States of America was suddenly and deliberately attacked by naval and air forces of the Empire of Japan." The United States was going to war.

At a joint session of Congress on December 8, 1941, President Franklin D. Roosevelt *(at podium)* asked the Senate and House of Representatives to approve a declaration of war against Japan. The two bodies agreed with the request almost immediately.

> **"I saw things I don't care if I never have to see again ... men scared and so exhausted and stunned they just sat and stared."**
>
> —Mack Morriss, reporter for the *Yank*, January 2, 1943

CHAPTER TWO

FIGHTING BACK

"We have taken a tremendous wallop, but I have no doubt about the outcome," Admiral Chester Nimitz said confidently as he took command of the Pacific Fleet in December 1941. Yet the United States would suffer more defeats in the coming months.

Spurred on by their success at Pearl Harbor, the Japanese invaded the U.S.-held Philippines on December 8. They took control of the archipelago (group of islands) six months later. At the same time, Japanese forces invaded and conquered Malaya (modern-day Malaysia) and the Dutch East Indies (modern-day Indonesia and New Guinea). They also seized Guam and Wake Island, as well as the Solomon Islands and the Aleutian Islands. These costly setbacks proved that even the mighty United States was not ready for war against a strong, determined, and experienced enemy.

Soon after its success at Pearl Harbor, the Japanese army invaded the Philippines. The army had the islands under control by mid-1942.

WHO'S TO BLAME?

The question of how Japan was able to successfully attack Pearl Harbor has caused great debate among historians. Some of them firmly believe that Roosevelt was anxious to get the United States into the war. They think he somehow encouraged the Japanese attack by purposely being hostile to them.

Other historians who study Japanese communications have accused the leaders in Washington, D.C., of purposely holding back messages from Japan. These messages might have allowed those in the Pacific to have some warning of the attack.

Yet most historians don't accept these views. Most believe President Roosevelt was as shocked and surprised as anyone by the Japanese attack. Instead, they blame the failure of what was supposed to be an excellent intelligence system. "The intelligence system, beset by human frailty, did not work," noted one writer. "President Roosevelt loved the Navy. He would not have allowed his precious ships and men to be sent to the bottom. That was not in his character."

The idea that the president was surprised and shocked by the attack is strongly supported by the United States' weak response in the early months of 1942. U.S. forces were not prepared for the quick Japanese advances that followed. Whatever the cause for the

Uniforms That Disappeared

Books about military history show many colorful photos of men who fought battles. Knights were in gleaming silver armor. Roman centurions wore bright metal breastplates. The British had their red coats and white pants. Soldiers through the ages strut through the history books looking like peacocks displaying their plumage. Yet these soldiers would not have lasted long in the jungle fighting on the islands in the Pacific.

In 1896 U.S. artist Abbott Thayer came up with the idea of applying the protective coloring of animals in nature to art. During World War I, an artist serving in the French army recommended the idea to his officers. A few countries tried to use what came to be called camouflage (clothing or coloring that helps soldiers blend in with their surroundings). However, camouflage was not all that common. It was most often used to disguise ships so that German submarines would not easily spot them.

Camouflage became a standard practice in World War II. It was used to protect troops from sniper fire and to better aid troops in laying traps for the enemy. In the thick jungles of the Pacific islands, wearing camouflage gave the U.S. troops a strategic advantage.

Because of its success in World War II, camouflage is something that is taken for granted in the modern military. Far from strutting like peacocks, modern troops aim to have a uniform that can't easily be seen.

Japanese attack, it changed many Americans' opinions about the war. The United States had no choice but to fight back.

Soon after the Japanese attack, Japan's ally Germany declared war on the United States. As a result, U.S. forces would be fighting not only in Asia but also in North Africa and Europe. U.S. troops hurried to these areas in 1942.

A NEW ENEMY

For the U.S. troops in Europe, the enemy was familiar. They had fought each other in World War I. The Americans fighting in the Pacific, on the other hand, were fighting a war of different strategies and tactics. They were fighting an enemy whose values were alien to them. For example, Japanese troops believed surrender was dishonorable. Rather than face the eternal dishonor of giving in to the enemy, they fought to the death. This attitude created some of the most serious problems U.S. troops would face in the Pacific.

In battle Japanese troops hung on to positions long after any other troops would have surrendered. They were trained by their leaders to be military machines. They were treated brutally during their training and, by some definitions, would be considered brainwashed. Americans had never come across this level of extreme devotion to duty. Lieutenant Colonel Kerry L. Lane noted that the marines faced "heavily dug-in Japanese troops determined to fight to the last man."

On the other hand, Japanese soldiers hated Americans who surrendered. They treated Allied prisoners barbarically, and thousands died in captivity. U.S. army lieutenant Gene Boyt learned firsthand how brutal the Japanese could be toward prisoners. Boyt was stationed on the Philippines when war broke out. The Japanese successfully overran Allied forces there. They trapped the Allies on the Bataan Peninsula, on Luzon, the Philippines' largest island. Seventy-five

Surrounded by their Japanese captors, U.S. soldiers and sailors surrendered at Corregidor, the Philippines, in May 1942.

thousand U.S., Filipino, British, and Australian troops finally surrendered after a long siege in April. (A second Allied force, on the fortress of Corregidor, held out until May.)

The siege had left the soldiers on the brink of starvation. But their ordeal was only beginning. The Japanese had set up a camp to hold the prisoners. The camp was about 100 miles from where the surrender took place. So over the next six days, the tens of thousands of starving soldiers were forced to march across the island in extreme heat and humidity.

The Japanese captors beat, tortured, and killed thousands of prisoners along the way. Boyt described one incident where a soldier refused to give up a personal item that a Japanese guard wanted. "The Japanese response was swift and direct," he wrote. "They beat the man terribly, continuing the punishment long after he was immobilized on the ground."

The journey became known as the Bataan Death March. More than six hundred Americans, five thousand to ten thousand

Filipinos, and many British and Australian troops did not survive the trip. The accounts from survivors of the Bataan Death March agree that the Japanese treated them horribly because their surrender was seen as a contemptible act.

GRIM DETERMINATION

Of course, no matter the beliefs of the enemy, no matter the difficulties, the marines, sailors, soldiers, and aviators in the Pacific theater knew what they needed to accomplish. The memoirs from U.S. troops clearly show the grim determination of those who faced the enemy. Their determination was captured in the press accounts of the time.

Reporter Mack Morriss was on the staff of the *Yank*. He wrote about the first time he saw this kind of fight—on Guadalcanal, an island in the Solomon Islands. "There were men who were filthy dirty and . . . tired. They were serious and, I think, mad. . . . I saw things I don't care if I never have to see again . . . men scared and so exhausted and stunned they just sat and stared."

During the Bataan Death March, U.S. prisoners of war created litters from blankets and poles to carry their wounded comrades, who had fallen along the roadside.

> **"We slept in our unwashed clothes, . . . showered in the rain, slept on the ground, and were forced to eat garbage."**
>
> —Marine George Lince, 1942

CHAPTER THREE

SERVING IN THE PACIFIC

The Allied leaders in the Pacific had a fairly simple overall strategy. U.S.-led forces would push the Japanese back to their homeland by taking control of selected Japanese-occupied islands. Not every island would be targeted. Some would be bypassed or hopped over. The strategy came to be called island-hopping.

To succeed, the Allies would be divided into two main forces. One force, under the command of U.S. Army general Douglas MacArthur, would begin in the southwest Pacific area (which includes Australia, New Guinea, and the Philippines). MacArthur's forces would move northward, gaining or regaining control of territory. Meanwhile, a second force, commanded by U.S. Navy admiral Chester Nimitz, was in charge of the rest of the Pacific. Nimitz would move westward from Hawaii "through the larger expanse of ocean and scattered islands such as Tarawa, the Mariana Islands and Iwo Jima."

The marines on board the naval vessels would be responsible for the land operations on those islands along the way. They would face the bloody task of invading and taking control of Japanese-occupied islands. Both wings of the advance would meet on the island of Okinawa, just 400 miles south of Japan. This would give them a good base from which to attack Japan.

The plan was simple. Making it a reality was a huge challenge. The strategy involved millions of soldiers, sailors, marines, and aviators. The army included the regular soldiers (or GIs), as well as the aviators who made up the U.S. Army Air Forces. (The U.S. Air Force was not created until September 18, 1947.)

The navy was more than just the sailors who served on the ships. It included the aviators who flew the planes on the big aircraft carriers and the marines who provided the land forces for the navy. The Seabees (the written-out nickname for the Construction Battalion, or CB) were

Members of the navy's Construction Battalion (or Seabees) spread asphalt during the creation of an air base. The Seabees were responsible for building airfields, bridges, and other structures quickly throughout the Pacific theater.

sailors who followed the marines. They built airstrips and other important structures once ground was gained by the fighting forces.

Altogether, about sixteen million Americans served in World War II. Of those, more than eleven million were in the army, which did the primary fighting in Europe and North Africa. The fighting in the Pacific involved mostly the remaining armed forces. This included just under five million U.S. naval personnel and marines.

THE DRAFT

The U.S. armed forces of World War II were mainly draftees (men obliged by law to serve in the military). Rather than wait for a declaration of war, a draft law was put into place right after the war began in Europe. All men eighteen to thirty-eight were subject to the draft.

After basic training, draftees learned skills that made them valuable to their units. Here, sailors check and repair instruments on a U.S. submarine.

In fact, at one point, men up to the age of forty-five could be drafted.

Before the Pearl Harbor attack, the U.S. government had placed many limits on the use of these draftees. For example, draftees served for only one year and only served within U.S. territory. Those limits were canceled after the attack on Pearl Harbor.

Ten million men were drafted to fight in the war and another six million signed up on their own. Roughly 405,000 of these troops died either in battle or from other causes during the war. Another 670,000 were wounded. For the first time in a conflict involving U.S. troops, the number of deaths from disease was less than the number of deaths from battle injuries. This was due to better medical services and access to antibiotics for treating infections.

Women in World War II

For the first time, women were active participants from the beginning of the conflict. Women weren't allowed in combat, but the various armed forces employed them in other important support jobs.

Women pilots enlisted in the U.S. Army's air corps. They didn't fly in combat, but they delivered planes and equipment in both theaters.

About 150,000 women served as members of the Women's Army Corps (WAC, or the WAAC—Women's Army Auxiliary Corps—as it was named in the early years of the war). An additional 80,000 served in the navy as WAVES (Women Accepted for Volunteer Emergency Service), making up almost 2.5 percent of naval forces.

Historian Judith A. Bellafaire noted: "Political and military leaders, faced with fighting a two-front war and supplying men and matériel [equipment and supplies] for that war . . . realized that women could supply the additional resources so desperately needed in the military and industrial sectors." Or, as it was put more simply on the recruiting posters, "Free a Man to Fight."

The women who signed up for the army were part of a separate unit, but the army provided all their lodging, food, uniforms, and medical care. They were paid, although not on the same pay scale as soldiers. By the end of the war, more than eight thousand women were in the WAVES, led by their own female officers. This was an amazing step forward for American women. It would have far-reaching effects in the years to come.

Women in the armed forces had a wide range of roles. They worked as clerks and typists and in communications, transportation, and intelligence. They worked as ordnance engineers, mixing gunpowder and loading shells. In the Pacific theater, they faced the same diseases as the troops. They got malaria from the ever-present mosquitoes and suffered from the brutal heat and humidity.

Women also continued to serve in the separate Army Nurse Corps, which had previously been the only job for women in the army. About fifty-nine

A U.S. Army nurse oversees patient care on Christmas Eve 1944 in the Philippines. The hospital is located in a church, where worshippers are also attending services.

thousand nurses served in the Army Nurse Corps. For the first time, their service was not limited to hospitals far behind the battle zone. Nurses were sent to work in field hospitals, including those in active battle zones, where they came under enemy fire. Many nurses earned Purple Hearts for wounds they received while caring for wounded troops.

One nurse remembered a bomb that hit the ward in which she worked. "The sergeant pulled me under the desk, but the desk was blown in the air, and he and I with it. . . . My eyes were being gouged out of their sockets, my whole body felt swollen and torn apart by the violent pressure." She was luckier than many of her patients. Parts of bodies and severed limbs were spread around the area.

> "The sergeant pulled me under the desk, but the desk was blown in the air, and he and I with it."
>
> —U.S. nurse describing a blast, 1942

An Unexpected Enemy

Women in the military, wherever they worked, faced an unexpected enemy. Some of the very soldiers and sailors they were helping were hostile to the nurses. Some historians say this happened because the troops wanted to return to their traditional world in the United States after the war was over. Troops couldn't believe that women would be willing to return to their traditional roles after having had so much freedom.

One survey of soldiers' letters home—done by the army's Office of Censorship—showed that 84 percent of the letters that mentioned women were generally against women being in the military. Vicious rumor campaigns about the behavior of women in the military were started. Letters sent home accused the women of bad

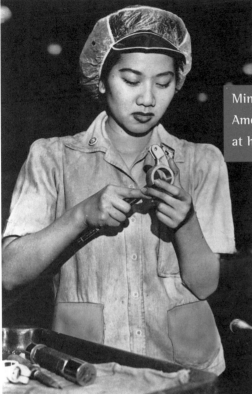

Minority women, such as this Asian American, contributed to the war effort at home by working in factories.

morals. Ironically, most of the hostile soldiers never even met a woman in the army. So, many of their feelings were not based on personal experiences.

What about the fears that women would reject their traditional roles after the war ended? History shows that the role of women did indeed change after World War II. They wanted to be more involved in the workforce and in society. But the pressures for these overdue changes were the same pressures that made women want to be part of the armed forces in the first place.

Women on the home front were making an important contribution to the war effort as well. Almost two million American women took over factory jobs, freeing men to serve in the military. The women earned fame when the character Rosie the Riveter became popular. Widely distributed posters of Rosie depicted the image of a strong woman. She represented women working as shipbuilders, steelworkers, lumber mill workers, and in other traditionally male jobs. As with the women serving in the armed forces, this caused a dramatic change in U.S. society after the war ended.

African Americans in World War II

African American troops also played a bigger role in World War II than in previous wars. Many of the roughly one million African American servicepeople served with merit. Benjamin O. Davis Jr. was the first African American to earn the rank of brigadier general in the regular army, although he was not awarded that rank until much later in his military career.

Lieutenant Colonel Davis was the commander of the Tuskegee Airmen, an all-African American fighter group that battled the Germans and Italians in the skies over Europe and the Mediterranean. The notable Tuskegee pilots and crews earned several firsts during the war. For instance, the group's 99th Pursuit

The famous Tuskegee Airmen made up the all-African American 99th Pursuit Squadron. The pilots fought in the European theater.

Squadron pulled off a remarkable feat when they destroyed five enemy aircraft in just four minutes.

The Tuskegee Airmen, like all African American military units, were segregated from the rest of the U.S. Army. They served in separate, blacks-only units. Segregation was common in the United States at the time. Segregating African American troops from white troops had been the policy of the U.S. military from the Civil War (1861–1865). So in World War II, the policy didn't change. The U.S. Navy had submarines with all–African American crews. (The U.S. military was finally integrated in 1948.)

One of the ways in which discrimination was most evident was with Congressional Medals of Honor, the highest military award a soldier could receive. A total of 431 Medals of Honor were awarded in World War II. Although African Americans received other honors, none achieved this one. President Bill Clinton corrected this wrong in 1997. He awarded the Medal of Honor to seven African American World War II veterans. Only one of them was still living.

NATIVE AMERICANS IN WORLD WAR II

Native Americans, especially the Navajo, played a critical role in the Pacific theater. About forty-four thousand Native Americans served in the armed forces during the war. Another forty thousand worked in defense industries. Those in the armed forces earned many awards for bravery, including three Congressional Medals of Honor. The Native Americans found a special place with the marines, who accepted them as fellow warriors. Despite all the individual efforts and bravery of the Native Americans, their greatest contribution was in the signal service as code talkers.

During World War I, the army had used a few Native Americans to send radio messages in the Choctaw language to confuse the Germans. The technique was so successful that military leaders in World War II expanded the program. It became one of the most successful tools in the Pacific. One historian noted that Navajo was a perfect secret code. It "is an unwritten language of extreme complexity...unintelligible to anyone without extensive exposure and training...one estimate indicates that less than 30 non-Navajos, none of them Japanese, could understand the language at the outbreak of World War II."

About four hundred Navajo code talkers served in the marines. They were trained in the military terms that were used to send out orders. Then they were assigned to marine units throughout the Pacific where their job was simply to talk to one another.

The Japanese were known for their ability to break codes. In fact, they broke the codes used by the U.S. Army and its air forces. Although they worked hard to break the Navajo code, they failed.

THE NAVAJO CODE

The marine Navajo code talkers *(below)* gave their units the most effective secret communication system possible in the Pacific campaign. They used an unsolvable code, known to a very small number of people. After the war, the Department of the Navy released the dictionary used by the code talkers to send their messages. The dictionary (available online at http://www.history.navy.mil/faqs/faq61-4.htm) provides a look at the complex messages that were sent by radio and telephone.

The code included words that represented letters (up to three words for the more commonly used letters in the alphabet). For example, WOL-LA-CHEE (ant), BE-LA-SANA (apple), and TSE-NILL (axe) represented the letter A. Since a message using that system would take too long to transmit and translate, common military words were also given coded translations. Thus a military corps would be indicated by DIN-NEH-IH, the Navajo word for "clan." A platoon was designated as HAS-CLIS-NIH, the Navajo word for "mud."

The code also allowed for officer designations. For example, commanding general was BIH-KEH-HE, or "war chief." Names of countries were in the code. The United States was NE-HE-MAH, or "Our Mother." Types of planes and ships showed up too. A fighter plane was DA-HE-TIH-HI, or "humming bird." Words designated locations and orders to field troops. The code was considered so secure that many of the words, such as *attack, capture,* and *conceal*, were translated directly into Navajo. The code talkers were admired for their simple and perfectly executed SILAGO-KEH-GOH HA-NEH-AL-ENJI, or "military making talk" (communication).

Being able to communicate secretly was a fantastic help to the marines. It allowed them to make plans without fear of being exposed. Many historians credit the code with some of the greatest marine victories in the Pacific.

LIFE IN THE MILITARY

Soldiers, sailors, marines, and aviators all dealt with issues that have plagued military forces for all time. They complained about either too many drills or not enough preparation. They complained about the food. They complained about the conditions of the camps. They complained about how few letters they were getting from home and how long it took to receive mail.

Homer Grantham served as a marine in the Pacific, and he noted the terrible food: "[A] diet of dehydrated eggs, dehydrated potatoes, and Spam. The Marines must have had the worst food in the Pacific. . . . The Seabees and the air force had the best food." Grantham said he even preferred the K rations (canned meals) the marines were given in the field to what they were fed behind the lines.

The World War II forces were the first to have scientifically produced rations. The K rations were quickly followed by C rations, which provided 3,700 calories a day. "Each ration weighed about 5½ pounds and was packaged in eight or nine small cans: Three of the cans (one for each meal) were M, or meat, units; three were B, or bread, units; one or two were for fruit; and one was for accessories, which included toilet articles and tobacco."

Although many soldiers complained about the lack of variety, this was a great improvement over what had been used in the past. In fact, the U.S. military still uses the same system. The food is called MREs (which stands for "meals ready to eat"), and there is more variety. However, because the food is less than tasty, some soldiers call MREs

UNINTENDED CONSEQUENCES

In World War II, the troops fighting the battles were nowhere near kitchens that could offer them hot food. The army used special K and C rations to keep them fed and equipped with supplies such as toilet paper. It also provided them with a new recreational habit.

Each package of rations included boxes for three meals. Each of those boxes included four cigarettes. The cigarettes were provided free by tobacco companies as their way of supporting the troops. A whole generation of soldiers came home from World War II addicted to cigarettes *(right)*. The same had happened in World War I, but a smaller percentage of American men had served then, so the impact was not as great.

Although some scientists warned that cigarettes were dangerous to the health of smokers, it was not a popular view at the time. The sailors, soldiers, marines, and aviators enjoyed their free cigarettes. Then they came home, unable to break the habit.

Iwo Jima

South China

AND

"meals rejected by everyone." No doubt many World War II troops felt the same about their own canned meals.

CAMP CONDITIONS

In addition to bad food, the U.S. troops had to deal with all the usual problems of being at war. U.S. Marine Kerry L. Lane, on Guadalcanal, spoke of his living area being "infested with mice and rats ... land crabs ... [and] red ants."

While serving in the Solomon Islands, these sailors decorated their barracks with posters and pinups of movie stars. Sack time was a favorite way to spend their few free hours.

Herbert Merillat, the historian for the First Marine Division, also had something to say about the rats on Guadalcanal. He wrote of one night's experience: "There were at least a dozen, chirping and scampering. The two sides of my bunk seemed to be their main thoroughfares. It's hard to sleep with their constant padding back and forth and squealings in your ears."

Soldier Floyd Radike complained that camp conditions were helping the spread of malaria and other diseases. George Lince summed up the living conditions, perhaps for all of the land troops, when he wrote: "We slept in our unwashed clothes, used an ineffective smelly liquid as an insect repellent, showered in the rain, slept on the ground, and were forced to eat garbage."

Letters from home also had a great impact on the lives of the troops serving so far away. Soldiers' accounts and diaries show long lists of complaints that were often followed by comments about not having received mail. In a letter to his wife, Ensign Jack Poultron captured the emptiness that missing letters meant to the troops. "No letters to be answering tonight—none since Friday. I have become spoiled wanting letters every day. The days are so empty when they don't come, those tenuous threads back to you."

The opposite was also true. The most positive comments about their experiences came when the troops were in contact with loved ones back home. Merillat wrote in his diary, "Got a nice stack of letters from the States. . . . That helps." Lince remembered: "Letters from my mother were newsworthy and a moral[e] builder."

It was a difficult time for all the troops who were far from home doing a hard job. It was, of course, also difficult on the ones waiting at home. Poultron's wife wrote of how lonely she was after he had been gone for seventeen months. "I need to see you. The days fall from us like dead leaves."

Men on a troop transport wait eagerly to hear their name called during mail call. Letters from home connected sailors and soldiers with their loved ones faraway.

> **"We were in new and threatening surroundings and we had all heard many stories of Japanese combat prowess."**
>
> —Lieutenant Colonel Kerry L. Lane, 1942

CHAPTER FOUR
WINNING ON LAND

Before the war, most Americans had probably never heard of the Pacific islands where the battles took place—Peleliu, Okinawa, Bougainville, Saipan, the Marianas, the Solomons, Guadalcanal, and Iwo Jima. During the war, Guadalcanal and Iwo Jima became well-known, important battle sites. They are both famous for the ferocity of the fighting, the difficulty of the terrain, and the willingness of the U.S. troops to stay with a difficult job until victory was theirs.

A HOSTILE ENEMY

As the Americans began their island-hopping offensive in August 1942, they did not know what they would find. Stories of the enemy had already become legends. Lieutenant Colonel Kerry L. Lane

In 1942 Japanese troops on Bataan celebrated their victory by yelling their war cry, banzai.

summed up the fears of all the soldiers as they landed. "We were in new and threatening surroundings, and we had all heard many stories of Japanese combat prowess."

Lieutenant Floyd Radike echoed these feelings. He said, "The Japanese had won the psychological warfare ... [with] their night attacks, their total disregard for their own lives, their yells and 'banzais,' and their patience in waiting for hours under a bush to kill one American."

Eighteen-year-old George Lince was shocked to realize that this enemy he faced had been trained and conditioned to *want* to kill him. As a U.S. soldier, he was trained to kill the enemy if he met him in battle. But it was not a personal hatred. It was a job that had to be done. In noting one difference between the Americans and the enemy, he said, "No one ever attempted to inflame my anger to kill." Added to the normal anxiety of a new soldier facing battle, this psychological factor was yet one more hurdle to overcome.

SHIPPING OUT

The troops were shipped out to bases in the Pacific on large transport ships (below) that carried as many as six thousand at a time. The trip was tedious. Most diarists mention the voyage just in passing, many not even giving the name of the ship they traveled on.

One ship, the USS Hermitage, was almost constantly under way starting in 1942. The ship made more than a dozen trips across the ocean, sometimes carrying troops bound for Europe, other times for the Pacific. A naval history points out that this converted luxury liner traveled "230,000 miles and transported 129,695 passengers" during the course of the war. The long rides on the crowded ships gave the soldiers much time to wonder what they would face upon arrival.

AMPHIBIOUS AND JUNGLE WARFARE

An attack on enemy shores by land and sea forces is known as an amphibious operation. Invading a heavily defended island was not easy. Just getting to shore could be deadly.

The attack usually began with a massive bombardment. Aircraft and naval guns pounded the target with bombs and artillery shells—sometimes for days. The idea was to soften up the Japanese defenses. (In reality, the Japanese were often dug in so deeply that the bombardments weren't effective.) Then the troops were sent in.

In most cases, soldiers arrived in landing craft. These flat-bottomed vessels could cross shallow waters, bringing soldiers close to the water's edge. The naval guns provided cover, and aircraft protected them from overhead. When the soldiers hit the beach, they were usually greeted by a hail of bullets.

Many of the marines were exposed to enemy fire for the first time. Russell Davis remembered his first landing at Peleliu Island in 1944. He felt alone and cut off from the rest of the world while "everywhere the air hummed and sang. The zip, zip, zip [of the bullets] became so steady it settled into one drone at high pitch. . . . I fell out of the water and on to the beach." He was not even aware

Marines and soldiers jump from landing craft to reach the beach at Guadalcanal, the Solomon Islands.

that he had been wounded as he made his way up the beach.

The first goal was to set up a beachhead (a secured landing spot). From there, the soldiers moved inland, clearing the island of Japanese soldiers. This was deadly jungle warfare, fought in hot, sticky, insect-filled conditions. "In the jungle," wrote one reporter, "a marine killed because he must, or be killed. He stalked the enemy, and [the] enemy stalked him, as if each were a hunter tracking a bear cat."

The jungle provided good cover for whichever side got there first. Troops knew they could be walking into an ambush with no warning and with no sign that enemy troops were nearby. Joseph McNamara came close to getting killed in one of those situations. "I had crossed an open area and got behind a coconut tree," he remembered. "I raised my head up and looked around the coconut tree, and the instant I raised my head to the right, a shot rang out."

On the other hand, the dense jungle fighting at least allowed the troops to dig in to protect themselves. This was not the case on Okinawa, however, an island made of coral. Coral is like rock. The U.S. fighters "could not get below ground by scooping out foxholes,

After coming through the jungle, U.S. soldiers cross a river on Bougainville, an island in the Solomons.

and thus were inviting targets for enemy riflemen and exposed to the flame and fragments of exploding mortar shells."

SECURING THE AIRSTRIPS

One of the most vital strategies of the island-hopping campaign was to secure each island's airstrips. The airstrips were needed to further the advance of the U.S. offensive. For example, Henderson Field on Guadalcanal was a crucial spot and thus hotly fought over by the Americans and the Japanese.

The United States invaded Guadalcanal on August 7, 1942. The attack was the first big step in the land war against Japan. U.S. troops gained a partially completed airfield and some of the land surrounding it. The Japanese then began a series of landings on other parts of the island to drive away the Americans. Six months of ferocious fighting followed.

War correspondent Richard Tregaskis described the scene after an attack along the Tenaru River as a "macabre nightmare." On the strip of land from which the Japanese had attacked, "we saw groups of [Japanese] bodies torn apart by our artillery fire, their remains fried by the blast of the shells. We saw machine-gun nests which had been blasted, and their crews shredded, by canister fire from our tanks."

Two months later, marine Abraham Felber described what it was like after a particularly intense few days of fighting. "The Marines had not had a drink for two days. Dead [Japanese soldiers] were lying all about in foxholes. The stench was awful," he wrote. When food and water was finally delivered to the marines, Felber witnessed a gruesome scene. He saw "worn out Marines...sitting in among the dead [Japanese]... eating hungrily of canned rations, while the shiny green blowflies buzzed and swarmed over the adjacent horribly bloated corpses."

> "The Marines had not a drink for two days. Dead [Japanese soldiers] were lying all about in foxholes. The stench was awful."
> —U.S. Marine Abraham Felber, 1942

The airfield on Iwo Jima, Japan, was fought over even more. It was one of the only islands in the area flat enough to be used as runways. To secure the island in February 1945, "Marines fought valiantly up a mountain bristling with enemy troops, bullets flying, bodies falling."

U.S. Marine Dave Severance described the marines' experiences on the island. "The troops faced a solid wall of reinforced concrete pill boxes," he remembered. Because of the terrain, each of the concrete machine-gun enclosures (pillboxes) had to be taken out

During the battle for Iwo Jima, marines fought in hand-to-hand combat.

individually. They were removed by "assault squads with demolitions and flame throwers." The U.S. assault troops, which had rifles and machine guns, tried to keep the enemy crouched down in the pillboxes. This way the troops could get close enough to attack. Even so, they faced "desperate conditions."

On Iwo Jima's Mount Suribachi, a group of soldiers and marines raised the American flag on February 23, 1945. It was, as one historian put it, "the first American flag ever to fly over Japanese home territory. It was more than just a proud moment; it was also an historic one."

COURAGE AND DETERMINATION

It would be impossible to tell every story of heroism shown by U.S. troops fighting on land in the Pacific. There are simply too many stories. Yet some stories stand out more than others.

TWO RAISINGS

Two flag raisings happened on Iwo Jima. An officer asked the unit to hand over the first flag *(below)* because he wanted to preserve it for history. The men were not willing to give it up. The flag symbolized their service to the United States. So the unit repeated the flag raising with another, larger flag. The image of that flag raising, captured by newspaper photographer Joe Rosenthal, is the one that became famous.

For the marines fighting on Iwo Jima, it seemed only right that they should be able to keep their flag. They had certainly paid for it with their own blood. Historians call Iwo Jima "the most costly battle in the history of the United States Marine Corps. With over 60,000 men participating in the campaign nearly a 40-percent casualty rate overall. Many line companies lost over 90 percent of their men."

Iwo Jima

Sergeant Joseph Julian of Sturbridge, Massachusetts, served with the marines on Iwo Jima. U.S. forces outnumbered the Japanese three to one, but the Japanese were in bunkers and pillboxes willing to defend their ground to the last man. The U.S. Marines started to attack in February 1945.

Eighteen days after the attack began, Julian decided to break through a defended position. Then his men could advance. Witnesses described how Julian crawled forward into the area between the U.S. position and that of the enemy. He then "demolished one four-man

Joseph Julian *(right)* earned the Congressional Medal of Honor for his daring one-man assault on Japanese-occupied trenches on Iwo Jima in March 1945.

strongpoint with two hand grenades, killing its screaming occupants... plunged to cover behind a boulder and emptied his carbine in a single burst, wiping out two more... got to his feet and dashed back for more ammunition to continue the furious one-man assault." Three hours later, the brave sergeant was dead from machine-gun fire in another attack.

The story of Corporal Al Schmid of Philadelphia, Pennsylvania, is another example of incredible heroism. Schmid was a machine gunner defending an area along the Tenaru River on Guadalcanal. At one point, Japanese troops launched a surprise attack.

The marines did their best to hold their position in the face of the assault. Schmid and his team kept up a steady stream of fire into the oncoming Japanese. Then a mortar shell hit their equipment and damaged the machine gun. It also blinded Schmid, doing permanent damage to his eyes. Despite his loss of vision, "he got the machine gun back into action and continued firing. His assistants coached him from target to target, adjusting fire by watching the flight of the gun's tracer bullets." Schmid earned the Navy Cross for his bravery under fire.

> "Vengeance will not be complete until Japanese seapower is reduced to impotence."
> —Admiral Chester Nimitz, 1942

CHAPTER FIVE

WINNING AT SEA

For five long months after the attack on Pearl Harbor, the Japanese appeared unstoppable. They moved freely through the Pacific, and more and more land fell under their control. Meanwhile, the U.S. Navy was busy regrouping. It was determined to win its first real battle against the Japanese.

The navy's first big opportunity came in May 1942 at the Battle of the Coral Sea. This was the first naval battle fought between aircraft carriers. Although the carriers were fighting one another, it was mainly the pilots, not the sailors on the ships, who did the attacking.

The U.S. and Japanese carriers—which were escorted by a group of other warships, including cruisers and destroyers—never came within visual range or actually fired one another during the battle. Instead, each side launched aircraft to attack the enemy carriers. The United States lost one aircraft carrier and a destroyer, and another carrier was damaged. The Japanese suffered similar damage.

The Battle of the Coral Sea was not a decisive battle. Most

Crew members climb down ropes from the U.S. aircraft carrier *Lexington,* which Japanese planes bombed during the Battle of the Coral Sea. Smoke hides the naval destroyer that waits to pick up the survivors. About 92 percent of the crew was rescued.

historians gave the advantage to the Japanese. In terms of morale, however, it was clearly a huge U.S. victory. After five months of retreat in the face of the Japanese offensive, the enemy had been stopped. More important, the Americans had used the battle as a chance to refine new strategies.

A WAR OF ATTRITION

In early June 1942, the two navies met again, near the island of Midway, about 1,100 miles north of Hawaii. By this time, the Japanese had lost most of their fear of and respect for the United States after a string of victories. The Japanese were convinced that the U.S. fleet was weak and faltering.

The Japanese saw an easy way to end the conflict. They planned to lure U.S. aircraft carriers into a trap and destroy them in a final, spectacular defeat. The Japanese began their attack with a bombing raid on Midway. But the U.S. code breakers found out about the plan, and Admiral Nimitz was ready to counterattack.

The Unites States caught the Japanese by surprise. In an aerial battle, U.S. pilots sank four Japanese carriers, while just one U.S. carrier was lost. The Japanese fleet experienced a crippling loss. By the time the battle was over, Admiral Nimitz could state with fervor, "Pearl Harbor has now been partially avenged." He proclaimed, "Vengeance will not be complete until Japanese seapower is reduced to impotence."

The victory gave the United States a much-needed morale boost. But more important, it established an effective strategy to use against the Japanese. Americans could produce replacement ships, planes, tanks, and weaponry at a rate with which the Japanese could not even begin to compete. The United States had

An aerial view of Midway Island shows the U.S. airfield that U.S. forces successfully defended in June 1942. The fiercely fought battle was the first decisive victory for the United States in the Pacific.

great resources and production skills. The United States waged a war of attrition. It methodically destroyed Japanese equipment to bring the war to a halt.

All but three of the twenty-one ships that were sunk or damaged in the attack on Pearl Harbor were fixed and put back into service. The United States

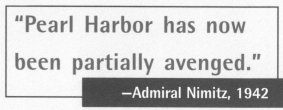

"Pearl Harbor has now been partially avenged."
—Admiral Nimitz, 1942

made aircraft carriers, destroyers, and submarines at an even faster rate. Japan's greatest weakness was a lack of matériel and personnel to match that production rate.

Losing four carriers—nearly half of its carrier fleet—was a major blow for Japan. Japanese strategy became more conservative. The United States had taken over the offensive in the Pacific. The end of the war was still three years away, but the tide had turned against the Japanese.

NAVAL VESSELS

The United States had a wide range of naval vessels in the Pacific, each with its own role. Aircraft carriers worked in tandem with battleships, destroyers, cruisers, troop transport ships, and minelayers. The U.S. Navy also had a large fleet of submarines, many of which saw heavy service during the last half of the war.

James J. Fahey was a seaman on the light cruiser USS *Montpelier.* He explained that his boat had a specific job off the coast of Guadalcanal. "Our job will be to bombard the [Japanese] on shore and prevent [Japanese] subs and warships from attacking our transports, minelayers and troops," he wrote. It was safer to be on a ship than fighting in the jungle (less than 1 percent of navy personnel died in battle compared to almost 3 percent of marines). But the duty still had

Landing ship, tanks (LSTs) were designed to transport troops and tanks and other vehicles. The ships' opened their giant doors into the surf to off-load men and supplies. From the beachhead, soldiers build a pier to speed up the operation.

its risks. Fahey noted that sailors were in trouble if their ship was attacked and sunk, "because if you land in the water the sharks will get you, and if you land on one of the islands the [Japanese] will get you."

Submarines first became a truly major weapon during this war. Statistics on their effectiveness are impressive. Although they made up only 2 percent of the ships in the U.S. Navy, submarines sank 30 percent of Japan's navy and almost 5 million tons of Japanese non-military shipping. Historians believe the biggest mistake made by the Japanese in their attack on Pearl Harbor was in focusing on the battleships instead of the submarines. *Jane's Naval History* notes, "The American submarine base was unscathed. Washington immediately ordered unrestricted submarine operation, all Japanese shipping being assumed to be supporting the military effort."

But the submarines' effectiveness came at a cost. The Japanese sunk fifty-two U.S. submarines during the war. Being trapped on a sinking sub was a virtual death sentence. Sailors on surface ships had at least a chance of survival if their ship sunk.

More than 3,500 men lost their lives on these underwater boats. In fact, this 2 percent of the navy suffered 10 percent of the navy's battle deaths. Perhaps this is why the accounts of the sailors serving on them are so powerful. The cramped and hot living conditions and dangers were the source of many stories. As one sailor described it: "You're scared. At least I always was. There are always so many unknowns. . . . Being in a small capsule deep in the ocean while presumably well-trained Japanese sailors were up there trying to kill you—that was not apt to bring on a sense of mental ease and repose."

Depth charges (explosives dropped into the water) were the submarine's main enemy. These devices could be set to explode at different distances below sea level. If they went off close enough to the submarine, they could damage or even sink it.

"The first depth charge exploded," wrote one submariner. "It was the loudest sound. . . . It was as solid as a blow to the skull, it was like a thunderclap between my ears. . . . It was as though a gigantic hand had reached under the sea, grabbed the Wolf [USS *Seawolf*] about the middle, and shaken her."

> "You're scared. At least I always was. There are always so many unknowns."
> —James Calverth, 1942–1945

Gregory Michno was on the USS *Pampanito*. He wrote about the glory of a successful attack, which was followed by the horror of being hit with "ash cans," the sailors' name for depth charges. "In the torpedo room the concussion from the exploding ship jolted the crew ... all smiled ... certain the attack was a success," he wrote. But then he described the long attack that followed as "pure hell. Down at six hundred feet or more, with water pressure at twenty tons [18 metric tons] per square foot ... [it] drove some men to the verge of madness."

Edward Beach was commander of the USS *Trigger*. He told a similar account of victory followed by terror. After landing four solid torpedo hits on an aircraft carrier, the sub dove and tried to get away. "Here they come and pul-lenty mad," he wrote. "It seems inconceivable that any machine ... can withstand such a vicious pounding. ... Two hundred feet [61 meters], and still the agony continues, the rain of depth charges ... increases in fury. ... We are scared."

The fear, however, was not as strong as the taste of success. Beach noted that after they were successful in an attack, "[I]t will take a lot of depth charges to dampen the spirits."

The submarine USS *Aspro* sinks a Japanese ship in June 1945.

The common theme in all the accounts is fear. The experience was exciting and terrifying for the submariners. During an attack, "Fear painted every man's face before he could try to wipe it off," remembered one writer. "The glassy sea had been great for sinking a tanker. It would be equally great for locating and blasting a submarine out of existence."

Of course, at the same time that Japanese destroyers were trying to wipe out U.S. submarines, U.S. destroyers were trying to sink Japanese submarines. John Williamson, executive officer on the USS *England*, wrote of a successful attack on a Japanese sub. He explained how it felt on his own ship. "Our little ship shuddered violently," he remembered. "Men throughout the ship were knocked off their feet. . . . [T]hat concussion was cataclysmic certainty that we had heard the last of the Japanese submarine."

THE KAMIKAZE

As with the submarines, the destroyers also faced their own special threats. Perhaps the deadliest one came near the end of the war, when the Japanese were desperately trying to stop the Allied advance on their homeland. The last months of the war gave rise to the kamikaze (Japanese suicide pilots). They tried to sink Allied ships by flying their airplanes straight into them.

Williamson recorded the first time "a Japanese fighter . . . came roaring out of the sky with its engine at top speed." This was a new and frightening weapon for the sailors on U.S. warships.

Ensign C. Snelling Robinson was on the destroyer USS *Cotton*. He watched from the deck as a Japanese plane "went into a steep dive on the light carrier *Princeton* and planted a five-hundred-pound [227 kilogram] bomb in the middle of the flight deck." It would not be his only sight of this new weapon.

Kamikaze pilots wore honorary ribbons during their suicide missions.

Robinson's ship successfully shot down another plane as it "dove on the *Ticonderoga*, crashing into the sea a few yards ahead of the speeding carrier." The crew of the *Cotton* saved the USS *Ticonderoga* that day. Their guns had hit the plane and made it "a flaming, uncontrolled meteor," so that it missed its target.

Who were these kamikaze pilots? After the war, several of those who trained as kamikazes but were never actually sent on a suicide mission wrote memoirs. One former pilot wrote about watching a close friend head off on a suicide mission, "Not a trace of anxiety on his face: neither excitement nor fear of death. . . . One would have thought he was about to leave on an ordinary training flight."

The author himself went on a suicide mission that failed to find its target because of weather. The pilot returned to base. His commanding officer arrested him for his failure. "It is as if you had deserted in the face of the enemy," the officer said.

The kamikaze had a formal ritual before his final mission. The pilot would "write final letters and, usually, a farewell poem . . . left a lock of hair or nail cuttings as mementos for his family. Then, inside the cockpit, he forgot himself as he aimed his craft at a target."

This form of honorable suicide, as it is sometimes called, had a long history in Japan. The attitude was similar to the Japanese troops on land who were determined to fight to the last man. The concept was as foreign to the U.S. sailor watching a plane come at his ship as it was to the U.S. Marine fighting the enemy in the jungle. The enemy would kill himself at a point when, by American standards, a rational man would surrender. How could U.S. troops understand the man who wrote to his parents, "Please congratulate me. I have been given a splendid opportunity to die."

Kamikaze attacks on U.S. ships were ultimately not effective. One historian noted, "The kamikazes were doing serious damage to the Allied fleet of merchant ships, more than was ever reported. But in comparative terms the kamikazes simply could not destroy enough ships to stop the American advance."

The sheer numbers and superior technology of the U.S. Navy proved to be most effective in slowly crushing the enemy. However, the Japanese spirit made them hang on much longer than anyone could have expected. This cost thousands of lives on both sides.

The USS *Kitkun Bay* shot down this kamikaze pilot before he could finish his bombing run. A later kamikaze succeeded in damaging the ship.

> "Never, during that time, had I felt any real, panic-stricken fear. Always I had faith that eventually I would get away."
>
> —Master Sergeant Gordon Manuel, 1943

CHAPTER SIX

WINNING IN THE AIR

Some of the most dramatic tales of World War II come from the pilots, whose acts were extraordinary at the time. Huge advances in flight technology since World War I had produced aircraft that could travel farther and faster than ever before. Planes were used as tactical tools in ways that were previously unimaginable.

Aircraft could bring the war to the enemy, even if the enemy was hundreds of miles away. U.S. fighters and dive-bombers attacked and sank Japanese warships and destroyed Japanese shipping, cutting off supplies to the homeland. In the later years of the war, as the Allies moved closer to Japan, U.S. bombers struck Japanese cities, destroying the nation's ability to make war matériel.

THE FATE OF PILOTS

Planes could be launched from aircraft carriers or from airstrips. Some pilots had exciting adventures while defending airstrips such as Henderson on Guadalcanal. Joe Foss made his first kill in 1942 when he shot down a Japanese Zero fighter (a lightweight aircraft). It almost cost him his own plane and his own life.

Foss was battling the Japanese in the skies over Guadalcanal when his engine gave out. As he tried to land, three Zeroes attacked him from behind. He remembered, "The Zeroes stayed right behind me and as I cleared the hill to land at Henderson they unloaded all their lead [bullets] at me." He managed to land safely but not before getting more than two hundred bullet holes in his plane.

Pilots, of course, wanted to get back to their airfield or aircraft carrier safely. But they often faced danger. Master Sergeant Gordon Manuel was on a B-17 bomber that was shot down. Of his eleven crew members, he was the only one to make it home alive. He made it to the nearby island of New Britain in spite of having a broken leg and shrapnel wounds. Unfortunately, the island held seventy thousand Japanese troops.

Joe Foss sits in the cockpit of his plane. He led many successful missions in the Pacific theater and was credited with shooting down twenty-six Japanese planes. His feat earned him the Congressional Medal of Honor and the Distinguished Flying Cross.

Manuel finally found a place to hide when he came upon a group of friendly locals. He stayed on the island for nine months, helping to rescue other pilots. He was finally rescued by a U.S. submarine. Manuel said of his ordeal: "Never, during that time, had I felt any real, panic-stricken fear. Always I had faith that eventually I would get away."

Sometimes the fate of downed pilots went well beyond adventure. They were scared of what would happen after they were shot down. In many cases, their fear was justified. "The Japanese made it a practice to shoot Allied pilots in their [parachutes] from the start of the war and never ceased the practice," noted one historian. Captain

Japanese soldiers escort a blindfolded U.S. pilot to prison. Many pilots feared the treatment they would receive if the Japanese caught them.

These pilots smile for the camera from the tail of a Hellcat fighter plane on board the aircraft carrier USS *Lexington* in 1943.

James Swett had to make a water landing after he lost his engine from enemy fire. After a successful landing he recalled, "there were two Zeros firing bullets into the water all around me."

In spite of their fears, pilots were well respected in the military. They faced grueling duty because there were few pilots and their training was long. John Howard McEniry Jr. was a Marine Corps pilot defending the airfield at Guadalcanal during the battle there. His unit had only eight planes, all two-man bombers. Because of the shortage of pilots, they flew from just before daylight until after dark. At a point when the island was under heavy attack, he remembered, "We all flew until we were exhausted.... [The] log book shows that we flew more than twelve hours.... [T]his was typical of all of us. The ground crews worked just as hard.... [Despite] our inadequate training, equipment and support ... we did do the job."

RAIDS ON TOKYO

Some of the pilots' feats served a valuable role in rebuilding the shaken morale of the American people. After the attack on Pearl Harbor and the growing Japanese presence in the Pacific, the U.S. public was scared of a possible attack on the mainland of the United States or of another on Hawaii. To boost morale, U.S. military leaders designed a daring plan to take the fight to the Japanese—if only for a few moments.

The plan was simple enough. The United States would send bombers to attack Japan's capital city of Tokyo. The purpose of the raid was not so much to do military damage to the country as to shock the Japanese and shake their feeling of superiority. But getting there would be the challenge. The closest U.S. airbase was thousands of miles from Japan. Even the longest-range U.S. bombers could only fly a few hundred miles.

One of the planes in the raid on Tokyo, Japan, takes off from the deck of the USS *Hornet* in April 1942.

LANDING A PLANE ON A POSTAGE STAMP

Aircraft carriers were a new and powerful weapon in the war in the Pacific. They allowed pilots to engage in battle in distant places by bringing their airfields with them. However, landing a plane on the deck of a carrier was not an easy task. It came with hazards much greater than landing on airstrips.

The pilots referred to it as landing on a postage stamp in the middle of the ocean *(below)*. This image captures the delicate and dangerous nature of a carrier landing. A pilot landing on a carrier is actually making a controlled crash landing. Carrier-based planes have a hook that catches a cable running across the deck. If the pilot catches the hook, he stops abruptly. If he misses it, he has to get airborne again before making another try. So the pilot has to land while still going fast enough to take off again. And takeoff is just as exciting. The planes are catapulted into the air from the carrier's deck.

The training to become a pilot was dangerous too. Pilots went through basic military training and primary flight training first. The pilots with the best skills were chosen for carrier pilot training. They were stationed on training carriers such as the USS *Wolverine* and the USS *Sable*. They trained there until they were skilled in taking off and landing on the carriers. About as many pilots died during training as died in combat.

Navy statistics show that about sixty thousand men completed aviator training during World War II. The best aviators were the aces. The aces could claim five or more kills (enemy planes shot down). Nineteen navy aviators are listed at the U.S. Naval Historical Center as winners of Congressional Medals of Honor in naval aviation for action in the Pacific during World War II.

Lieutenant Colonel James H. "Jimmy" Doolittle was a famous U.S. pilot of the time. The U.S. military assigned him the task of organizing the April 1942 raid. Doolittle decided to transport the B-25 airplanes by strapping them to the runway of an aircraft carrier, the USS *Hornet*. But taking off from the ship was extremely dangerous. These heavily loaded planes were made to take off on long airfield runways, not short aircraft carrier decks.

The sixteen planes, each carrying four 500-pound bombs, managed to take off, just barely getting airborne before clearing the flight deck. A short time later, they attacked Tokyo in broad daylight, just after noon. The bombers caused little damage. But the raid—the first attack on Japanese soil in almost seven hundred years—achieved its goal of shocking the Japanese population.

Three years later, the Japanese shock turned to horror. Once U.S. forces had captured airfields within bombing range of Japan, the U.S. Army Air Forces launched a massive campaign of destruction. Beginning in March 1945, U.S. bombers carried out devastating raids over Tokyo. Waves of B-29 Superfortress bombers dropped thousands of incendiary (fire-causing) bombs, starting massive fires.

Incendiary bombs burned trees and buildings throughout Tokyo in 1945.

The decision to use these bombs was controversial because they did more than military damage. These bombing runs targeted civilian populations, causing tens of thousands of deaths. The emperor of Japan had called on his people for their help in defending Japan. "Every Japanese citizen, man, woman, and child, young or old, was a soldier in the defense of the homeland." Historian Hermann Knell noted, "Women and children took training in opposing the invaders when and if they were coming."

Incendiary bombing was an effective military tactic. It was directed to where it would cause the most damage: "on a twelve-square-mile area of the most densely populated part of the city, where house[s] of wood, bamboo, and plaster crowded each other. . . . [T]he fires spread rapidly and the results were devastating."

One estimate stated that the incendiary bombing destroyed about 43 percent of the sixty Japanese cities that were targeted. The bombing, in Knell's words, "flattened an area thirty times larger" than that destroyed by the atomic bombs used later at Hiroshima and Nagasaki. A newspaper account described one of the attacks. "Flames visible for 60 miles rose from industrial Nagoya's nine square miles after more than 500 Superforts, the biggest B-29 armada ever sent against a single target, dropped 3,500 tons of incendiary bombs May 14 in the heaviest and most concentrated fire raid in history."

Airpower continued to play a major role in the conflict until the war's end. But the war could not have been won in the air alone. The victories on land and sea were equally crucial in destroying Japan's ability to conduct the war. Yet the fight in the air permanently changed the approach to war. For some of the early victims, who had been taken prisoner soon after Pearl Harbor, the sight of U.S. planes in the air was the only sign that they would be rescued.

> " We existed in spite of...the lack of any consideration...for our needs as human beings."
>
> —Major John M. Wright Jr., recalling his experience as a POW in World War II

CHAPTER SEVEN

PRISONERS OF WAR

The United States had not had to face the horrors of prisoner of war camps when the Americans fought in France in World War I. Some Americans did become prisoners of the Germans during World War II. Their situation, however, was not as dire as the one that faced prisoners of the Japanese. U.S. prisoner of war Major John M. Wright Jr. was held for more than three years. He summed up the experience: "We existed in spite of the bad treatment, the filth, the lack of water, and the lack of any consideration on the part of the Japanese for our needs as human beings."

The stories are truly horrible. Each account reinforces the stories of the others held prisoner by the Japanese. "I weighed about 180 lbs. when I was captured, and 98 lbs. when I was liberated," stated American prisoner of war John Emerick. "I survived, I think, because I built up such a hatred." Emerick still suffered from nightmares about his captivity fifty years later.

Private Andrew D. Carson called his memoir *My Time in Hell.* It is clear that for many of the captives, the experience was certainly that. Carson himself recalled being told that disobeying the captors' orders would result in being "severely punished until dead."

RULES OF WAR FOR PRISONERS

Rules accepted under international agreement were supposed to protect prisoners of war from brutality. The rules are often referred to as the Geneva conventions (the document and later

Freed U.S. prisoners of war (POWs) line up inside their former prison camp in Manila, the Philippines. They'd spent three years as POWs before Allied victories liberated the islands and the men.

ammendments relating to the treatment of prisoners of war that was in effect during World War II). The rules say that prisoners of war must be treated humanely. They are to be given adequate housing, food, and clothing, equal to that of a country's own troops. They are not to be tortured, and prisoners who surrender are not to be killed. These rules are often broken, especially in the heat of battle.

The experiences of U.S. prisoners during World War II were especially horrifying in the Pacific theater. They were held in captivity under inhumane conditions for a long period of time, with little hope of rescue until the war ended. The numbers of deaths exceeded the norm for other conflicts and other prisoner situations.

Various sources say that the Japanese took about 140,000 Allied troops as prisoners. Anywhere from 25 to 50 percent of those died while imprisoned. One prisoner noted that only one in three of the prisoners he knew survived. In comparison, the death rate among Allied prisoners

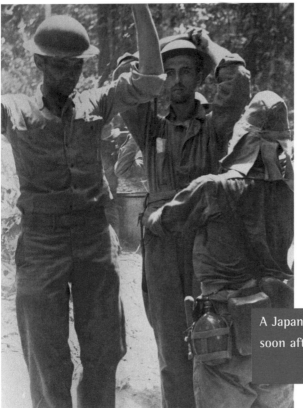

A Japanese soldier searches POWs soon after their capture.

STATISTICS ON
U.S. PARTICIPATION IN WORLD WAR II

Population of the United States:

133,500,000

Number of U.S. troops:

16,353,700

Percentage of troop participation:

12.2 percent

American deaths in combat:

292,131

Other deaths (disease, accident, etc):

115,185

Wounded:

670,846

Death rate:

2.6 percent

Overall casualty rate:

6.6 percent

Source: U.S. Department of Defense

held by the Germans in the same war was around 2 percent.

Major Wright was captured after the Battle of Corregidor, which occurred early in the war. He detailed a specific instance of "a horrible, forty-seven day voyage, during which our group was cut from over 1600 men to about 500."

Bataan Death March Prisoners

Some soldiers endured the Bataan Death March. This was a 100-mile journey that started where the troops surrendered and ended at the prison camp where they were held. Most of the march was on foot. Toward the end, the prisoners were transported by train.

Emerick remembered that the prisoners were "jammed ... in so tight that if somebody died you didn't know he was dead till after they let you out." Preston John Hubbard also survived the siege at Bataan. His description is equally chilling. "Shooting or bayoneting stragglers and the fallen seems to have been the rule rather than the exception."

Prisoner Herbert Zincke blamed this mistreatment on the fact that "American and Filipino soldiers on Bataan had cost the Japanese 10,000 casualties and five months of combat." This was combined with the

POWs covered their heads against the hot sun in a Japanese prison camp.

idea that "we had surrendered—not a normal or honorable course for a Japanese soldier." Another prisoner blamed the mistreatment on racial issues. He stated that the Japanese "regarded all Americans as just a bunch of mongrel dogs, a much lower class than the Japanese."

Yet another prisoner believed that since the Japanese were brutal with their own soldiers in training them, "it is not surprising that they abused and murdered enemy captives." He explained that the Japanese expected those subordinate to them to give "complete obedience . . . even if instructed to carry out suicide attacks." Prisoners were about as subordinate as anyone could get. In the eyes of their Japanese captors, they were "undeserving of respect."

Prisoners also had to live with the very real fear that they would be punished whenever the U.S. troops were successful in battle. Hubbard noted, "The Japanese generally punished American POWs after each raid . . . [with] physical beatings and a lowered living standard."

PERMANENT WOUNDS

For many U.S. prisoners, their physical wounds would be with them for the rest of their lives. Eugene Cunningham was a marine private who spent forty-four months as a Japanese prisoner. At one point, he was hit on the head with a claw hammer as punishment. His brother Chet collected POWs' accounts in memory of Eugene, who died in 1998. He said that Eugene's injuries plagued him all his life.

Several prisoner accounts detail the long-term psychological impact of their time spent as prisoners of war. Chet Cunningham quotes the experience of Major Robert M. Brown, who came across a particularly cruel Japanese interpreter while held in a prison camp. The interpreter, Mr. Ishihara, "hated Americans and his actions were those of a maniac. . . . I doubt that I will ever recover from the hatred I felt and still feel for Mr. Ishihara. . . . He still lives in my nightmares."

Andrew Carson wrote of being able over time to live with the physical horrors of life as a POW, "the continual sickness, the starvation . . . even the brutality." However, he and the others could not get used to "the psychological and emotional whirlpool we were thrown into." Wrote one prisoner of their nightmare, "Helpless to intervene for fear of suffering the same fate, we watched in horror as they butchered men before our eyes."

No wonder that the horrors of their experiences stayed with them long after the war ended. Especially for those in captivity for almost four long years, it seemed as if their lives would never be normal again.

> "Helpless to intervene for fear of suffering the same fate, we watched in horror as they butchered men before our eyes."
> —prisoner of war, 1942

FREEDOM AT LAST

As the war ended, prisoners were freed from their camps. Many needed immediate medical care before they could return home to the United States. Arriving home they received their back pay of $1 per day for food rations. This is what they would have been given were they not prisoners. They also received a bonus of $1.50 per day of captivity. This was considered reimbursement for the slave labor they had to do as prisoners.

Many POWs say they survived because they cooperated with one another and tried to help one another. Their loyalty to one another still exists, even as the numbers of survivors dwindle.

POW groups have fought hard for recognition by the U.S. government of their claims of abuse and for justice from the Japanese.

TOKYO ROSE

Propaganda—information (often false) put forth to support a specific cause or point of view—has always been a part of warfare. In World War II, technology changed the way propaganda was delivered. The Japanese, for example, used radio broadcasts from Tokyo Rose to send out their propaganda.

Tokyo Rose was not a real person. The Japanese gave the name to about a dozen females whom the government used to broadcast propaganda to U.S. troops. The job of the Tokyo Roses was to undermine American willpower. They talked about how great the Japanese were and how U.S. soldiers would all die far from home. They would claim victories that didn't exist. They exaggerated U.S. losses to make it look like Japan was winning the war.

Even though no real person called Tokyo Rose existed, an American woman of Japanese descent was tried and convicted of being her. Iva Toguri *(below)* was visiting Japan when war broke out. Not allowed to return home, she supported herself as an announcer but refused to say anything that could be used against the United States. U.S. military commanders agreed that she had done no harm to the U.S. cause.

After the war, however, Toguri was put on trial in San Francisco and was convicted of treason. Historians agree that Toguri had been the victim of wartime racism. Some of the witnesses against her confessed later that they had lied under oath. Toguri served six years in prison for being in the wrong place at the wrong time. Her name was only cleared in 1977 when President Gerald Ford granted her request for a presidential pardon.

TOGURI,
IVA
NO. 1
SUGAMO PRISON

War crimes trials were held after the war. Japanese political and military leaders were convicted of crimes against humanity. Seven leaders were sentenced to death. Sixteen others were sentenced to life in prison.

Many prisoners who survived cruel and inhumane treatment in the camps still believe that too few of the Japanese were held responsible for their crimes. They say it is insulting to the memory of those who suffered as prisoners of war.

CHAPTER EIGHT

THE ULTIMATE WEAPON

"As Mrs. Nakamura stood watching her neighbor, everything flashed whiter than any white she had ever seen. . . . [S]omething picked her up and she seemed to fly into the next room over the raised sleeping platform, pursued by parts of her house."

At two o'clock on the morning of August 6, 1945, Colonel Paul W. Tibbets, pilot of the *Enola Gay*, took off with his crew on a special mission from the island of Tinian in the Marianas. The *Enola Gay* carried a new kind of bomb—the atomic bomb. Its target was the city of Hiroshima, Japan.

Arriving over Hiroshima, the bomber dropped Little Boy (the code name for the bomb) over the city at 8:16 A.M. Seconds later, it detonated, causing a massive explosion and a mushroom cloud that

The city of Hiroshima is in ruins after an atomic bomb was dropped there on August 6, 1945.

rose 20,000 feet in the air. Within a few minutes, eighty thousand people died and 80 percent of the city was destroyed. Another sixty thousand Japanese died during the next several months from radiation poisoning. This devastation resulted from a decision that still remains controversial more than sixty years after the end of World War II.

SHOULD THE ATOMIC BOMB HAVE BEEN USED?

The controversy involves whether Japan would have surrendered without the arrival of the *Enola Gay* at Hiroshima and the arrival of the *Bockscar*, with the bomb nicknamed Fat Man, at Nagasaki on August 9, 1945. Even within the military community, some believe that President Harry S. Truman should have waited longer before ordering the bombing. Historian Gar Alperovitz quotes Admiral

A dense column of smoke rises thousands of feet above the Japanese port of Nagasaki on August 9, 1945.

Ernest J. King on this issue: "Had we been willing to wait," King said, "the effective naval blockade would...have starved the Japanese into submission through lack of oil, rice, medicines, and other essential materials."

Other historians present strong arguments that Japanese leaders knew they had lost the war. The historians claim Japan had been given ample opportunity to surrender and refused to do so. As in other issues in the war, from the treatment of prisoners to the use of kamikaze pilots, Japan's decisions reflected the major differences in the Japanese and American cultures. One historian noted: "[General] LeMay and XXI Bomber Command had brought Japan to its knees—but it would not surrender."

SAVING AMERICAN LIVES

U.S. leadership in the Pacific was planning to invade Japan for "what promised to be one of the bloodiest struggles in human history." Many of the Allied troops who had succeeded against Germany in Europe in May 1945 were being sent to the Pacific to fight against

Japanese emperor Hirohito *(front)* tours a destroyed section of Tokyo during the war.

Japan. The U.S. forces planned to begin the invasion on November 1, 1945. Japan had promised full resistance. Their motto was "One hundred Million Will Die for Emperor and Nation."

Various estimates predicted more than one million casualties among Allied forces if Japan was invaded. Intelligence showed that Japan was making "preparation for extensive use of suicide attacks." Kamikaze attacks were expected to increase in number as the attack on Japan neared. The Japanese military was placing mines (explosives) along shore areas to hinder the invasion. There was also talk of "piloted suicide torpedoes (*kaiten*) and preparations for using oil and gasoline incendiary devices."

GRIM DETERMINATION

U.S. troops were ready to accept the possibility of invading Japan. But they would also be quite happy to have something happen that would make it unnecessary. At its simplest, the U.S. troops fully expected that they and many of their comrades would die if the invasion occurred. They expected that more of them would be killed while invading Japan than had died in the entire war so far.

Lieutenant Floyd Radike knew the invasion was coming and was not very eager. But he described himself and his fellow soldiers as filled with "grim determination" to complete the work they had been doing, to "destroy, to the last man, if necessary, the military apparatus."

Soldier Paul Veatch thought he had seen enough of the Japanese to be "convinced that there would be no surrender.... The Japanese soldier would glory in sacrifice.... All warfare

The soldiers in the Pacific theater looked with grim determination at the possibility of invading Japan.

to date . . . would seem insignificant compared to . . . when the Japanese fought . . . on their home soil."

It is, of course, impossible to know what would have happened if the atomic bombs had not been dropped. Perhaps Japan would have eventually surrendered. Perhaps the fact that the Soviet Union declared war on Japan on August 8, 1945, and invaded Manchuria would have convinced Japanese military leaders that it was time to surrender.

Whatever forced the issue, it was the Japanese emperor Hirohito who ultimately urged the surrender. In a response that was very much in keeping with Japanese beliefs of the time, many of the military leaders committed suicide rather than take part in the surrender. The surrender took place anyway.

On September 2, 1945, the Japanese foreign minister Mamoru Shigemitsu *(seated)* signed the surrender documents aboard the USS *Missouri.*

THE SURRENDER

On September 2, 1945, Japanese leaders stood on the deck of the USS *Missouri,* which was anchored in Tokyo Bay. There they signed the surrender documents. President Truman declared V-J day (for Victory in Japan), and the world celebrated. The war was finally over.

PRIVATE EDDIE SLOVIK EXECUTED FOR DESERTION

On January 31, 1945, Private Eddie Slovik *(below right)* faced a firing squad. He became the only U.S. soldier executed by U.S officials during World War II. He also earned the distinction of being the first U.S. soldier executed for desertion since the Civil War.

Discipline is critical in a military organization, and several offenses are considered serious enough to merit the death penalty. Desertion—abandoning one's unit without permission for more than thirty days—is one of them. If one soldier is allowed to shirk his duties, it opens the way for others to try the same thing. Thus desertion is viewed as a grave offense.

Slovik was not the only soldier convicted of desertion in the war. More than twenty-one thousand soldiers were convicted. He was not even the only one sentenced to death. Forty-nine others received the same sentence but had their sentences changed to imprisonment. Slovik was executed by direct order of the supreme commander of the Allied armies, General Dwight D. Eisenhower, to serve as an example for all soldiers.

Slovik was not a typical U.S. soldier. As a boy, he had spent time in prison for theft. He believed his prison record would protect him from military service. Once drafted, he constantly asked for a noncombat position. He did not do well in training and left his unit in August 1944. Canadian forces found him and returned him to his unit in October. After being warned about the penalties for repeating his offense, he promptly deserted again. The army had seen an increase in military absences without leave. Many members of the general staff believed the problem would become much worse if they did not make an example of someone. Slovik was chosen to be the example.

Since the war ended, many presidents have been asked to pardon Slovik for his actions, but they have chosen not to do so. Some supporters still work to obtain a pardon for this soldier who faced death by firing squad to avoid death in battle.

An article in *Stars and Stripes* described the reaction among U.S. troops on Okinawa. When they heard that the Japanese had asked for peace terms, "American troops went wild.... [T]hey fired off guns and flares. Tracers filled the sky. Men yelled and beat on buckets. They hammered on one another's backs shouting—'the war's over.'" For men who had thought that death awaited them in the coming attack on Japan, this was the most welcome news possible.

However, for some Japanese soldiers, the war would not be over for many years. Several groups refused to surrender. One group of thirty-three soldiers on Peleliu Island, led by Lieutenant Ei Yamaguchi, attacked marines more than a year after the war ended. They finally surrendered in April 1947.

In 1995 NBC's news program *Dateline* interviewed Yamaguchi. When asked why he had not surrendered, Yamaguchi answered, "We couldn't believe that we had lost. We were always instructed that we could never lose. It is the Japanese tradition that we must fight until we die, until the end."

> "We couldn't believe that we had lost. We were always instructed that we could never lose. It is the Japanese tradition that we must fight until we die, until the end."
>
> —Lieutenant Ei Yamaguchi, 1995

The story of Second Lieutenant Hiroo Onoda is even more amazing. Onoda hid out on Lubang Island in the Philippines with a corporal and two privates. Japanese military leaders instructed them to stay in hiding no matter how long it took, because it might be several years before the country would again be able to fight back.

Carrying his sword, Hiroo Onoda surrenders in 1974, nearly thirty years after World War II ended.

Hiding from searchers, Onoda kept his small team trained and ready for combat. Onoda was the last survivor. He did not surrender until March 1974, nearly thirty years after the end of the war. This might seem shocking, but to those who fought against the Japanese in World War II, it is not the least bit surprising.

> "Our debt to the heroic men and valiant women in the service ...can never be repaid. They have earned our undying gratitude."
>
> —President Harry S. Truman, 1945

CHAPTER NINE

WINNERS AND LOSERS

When the war ended, the POWs were freed from captivity. The ships carrying soldiers, sailors, marines, and aviators came home to end their service. World War II became a subject for historians to analyze. Like World War I, it was remembered for unfinished business.

World War II actually achieved more than World War I did. The United Nations (UN)—a more effective international organization than the old League of Nations—was put in place. The UN has not always been the effective tool that many hoped for. But it has given all nations a forum in which to discuss a wide range of issues. It also provides a process to resolve at least some disputes between nations.

Troops wave from the deck of the transport ship bringing them back to the United States after their service in the Pacific theater.

Germany, Italy, Japan, and other losing nations received financial help from the victors to rebuild their countries. The world had learned a lesson after World War I. This time the defeated countries did not face humiliation and economic difficulties that could lead to future wars. The assistance from the Allies helped the defeated gradually become friendly with their past enemies.

Ironically, the United States ended up with unresolved issues with its ally the Soviet Union. The end of World War II led immediately to the cold war. This conflict involved disputes with the Soviet Union but never led to direct military action between the two countries.

AFTERWARD

The groups of Americans who supported the country's military efforts achieved a great deal on the domestic front. Women, African Americans, and Native Americans had offered their services and participated in defending the United States. They came home determined to make their own complaints heard. These groups fought for equal rights during the decades following the war. Although the struggle for civil rights took time and caused tension, the movement's members ultimately won the rights they sought.

In general, the World War II troops benefited from their service in the postwar period. The veterans of World War I had felt neglected by their own government after they came home from the war. These same veterans made sure that the veterans of World War II would have

Veterans and others marched against civil rights abuses in 1946.

many more opportunities than they had been given. Through the GI Bill, passed by Congress in 1944, members of the armed forces received help from the U.S. government. Substantial educational benefits were available if they chose to use them. Housing benefits were also provided through special veterans' home loans.

When the troops returned home, they were greeted with joy and the grateful thanks of the nation. The United States had become a major force on the international scene because of their efforts. Coming out of Pearl Harbor, stunned and unprepared, the United States had proved itself capable of not only rebounding from defeat but of leading the world to victory. President Harry S. Truman spoke for the whole country when he praised what U.S. troops had accomplished. "Our debt to the heroic men and valiant women in the service of our country can never be repaid," he said in an address to Congress. "They have earned our undying gratitude."

Few would have said at the beginning of the war that its ending would result in the United States becoming a superpower. U.S. technological and industrial capabilities—coupled with the courage, heroism, and determination of its troops—allowed the United States to help save Europe at the same time it defeated Japan.

A NUCLEAR WORLD

The victory created its own problems. The new atomic bomb technology raised world fear to new levels in the decades following the war. Atomic weapons and their successors, nuclear weapons, could actually destroy all life on Earth. Many people in the United States and around the world began to wish that nuclear weapons had never been developed. However, most people recognized that the fear caused by the new weapons had benefits. It kept some nations without nuclear technology from attacking other countries.

CLASSROOM FOR HIGH OFFICE

What do John Kennedy, Lyndon Johnson, Richard Nixon, Gerald Ford, and George H. W. Bush have in common? Besides all becoming U.S. presidents, they all fought in the Pacific theater in World War II.

Dwight D. Eisenhower was supreme commander of the Allied forces in the European theater of war. He came home to be the thirty-fourth president of the United States, serving from 1953 to 1961. The presidents after him used their service in the Pacific to help them gain a reputation for coolness under fire and for leadership that would take them to the White House.

John F. Kennedy *(at right, far right)*, thirty-fifth president, was the hero of PT-109, saving members of his crew when a Japanese destroyer sunk their boat in the Solomon Islands. Lyndon Johnson, thirty-sixth president, served as President Roosevelt's eyes and ears in the Southwest Pacific. Richard Nixon, thirty-seventh president, was in the supply corps in the U.S. Navy in the South Pacific. Gerald Ford, thirty-eighth president, served on an aircraft carrier, the USS *Monterey*, that saw substantial service during the war. George H. W. Bush *(at left)*, the forty-first president, was a medal-winning fighter pilot and war hero who earned the Distinguished Flying Cross.

All of them came home from war. Some went right into politics. Others pursued careers in business. All of them went on to become members of the most exclusive club of all, the U.S. presidency.

Like World War I, World War II was not a war to end all wars. Just a few years later, another war erupted, this time in Korea. In the Korean War (1950–1953), a U.S.-led UN force supported South Korea against Soviet- and Chinese-backed North Korea. Many of the troops who fought in the Korean War were World War II veterans.

REMEMBERING THOSE WHO FOUGHT

World War II has been remembered in many books and movies. Some of them are glory filled and unrealistic. Others are disturbingly accurate in their depiction of the horrors endured by the generation that fought around the globe.

In 2004 this greatest generation, as it is often called, was honored with a new memorial on the National Mall in Washington, D.C.

The Pacific Pavilion at the National World War II Memorial in Washington, D.C., honors those who fought, died, and worked to end the conflict.

THE GREATEST GENERATION

The soldiers, sailors, marines, and aviators who fought for the U.S. military in World War II are reaching the end of their lives. Historians are making an effort to see that the accomplishments of this greatest generation are not forgotten. They have an impressive monument on the National Mall in Washington, D.C. Their story has been told in countless movies that dramatize their heroic exploits. They are the benchmark against which modern troops and modern wars are judged.

For the people who fought the war in Europe, the battlefields are still there. In the Pacific, they are harder to find. But the veterans are remembered by the generations who still know them and who are trying to capture their stories before it is too late.

At the dedication of the National World War II Memorial on May 29, 2004, President George W. Bush said that this greatest generation "served bravely, fought fiercely and kept their honor—even under the worst of conditions. . . . [T]hey gave the best years of their lives to the greatest mission their country ever accepted."

There were thousands of veterans at that dedication ceremony. They were proud to have their president acknowledge the gift they gave their country. One veteran, former senator Bob Dole, said that the memorial "kept faith with our comrades from a distant youth." For a day, all of the United States remembered.

Marines pause during the fight to recapture Guam.

Located between the Washington Monument and the Lincoln Memorial, the National World War II Memorial greets visitors with the following words:

> Here in the presence of Washington and Lincoln, one the eighteenth century father and the other the nineteenth century preserver of our nation, we honor those twentieth century Americans who took up the struggle during the Second World War and made the sacrifices to perpetuate the gift our forefathers entrusted to us: a nation conceived in liberty and justice.

It is a fitting tribute to the sailors, soldiers, marines, and aviators who brought the United States back from the shock of Pearl Harbor to complete victory in a worldwide conflict. It is also a fitting companion to the bookends of war resting in and on the waters of Pearl Harbor today.

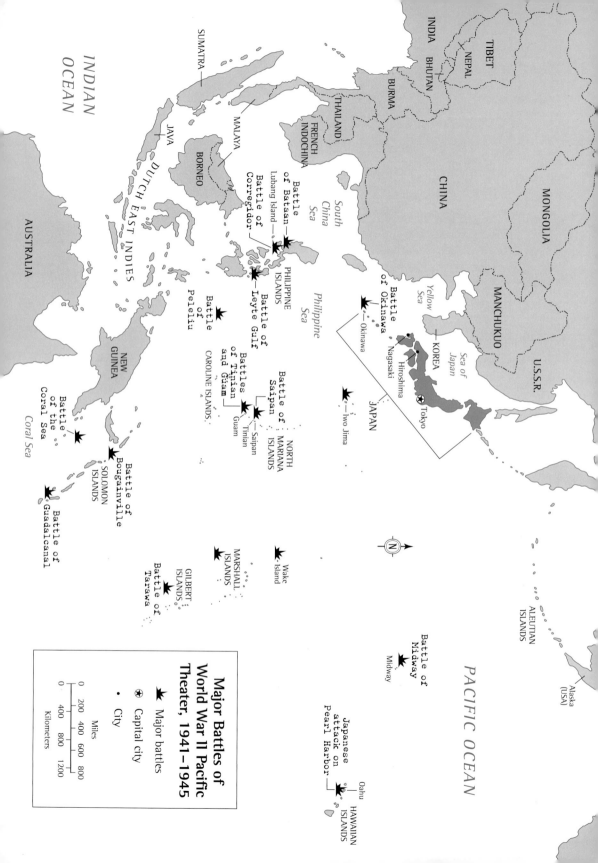

Major Battles of World War II Pacific Theater, 1941–1945

★ Major battles

⊛ Capital city

• City

Miles
0   200   400   600   800

Kilometers
0   400   800   1200

INDIAN OCEAN

PACIFIC OCEAN

SUMATRA

INDIA

BHUTAN

NEPAL

TIBET

BURMA

THAILAND

FRENCH INDOCHINA

MALAYA

JAVA

BORNEO

DUTCH EAST INDIES

AUSTRALIA

NEW GUINEA

CHINA

MONGOLIA

MANCHUKUO

U.S.S.R.

KOREA

JAPAN

Tokyo

Hiroshima

Nagasaki

Sea of Japan

Yellow Sea

South China Sea

Philippine Sea

Coral Sea

Coral Sea

Battle of Bataan

Battle of Corregidor

Lubang Island

PHILIPPINE ISLANDS

Battle of Leyte Gulf

Battle of Peleliu

CAROLINE ISLANDS

Battle of Okinawa

Okinawa

Iwo Jima

Battle of Saipan

NORTH MARIANA ISLANDS

Battles of Tinian and Guam

Guam

Saipan

Tinian

Battle of the Coral Sea

Battle of Bougainville

SOLOMON ISLANDS

Battle of Guadalcanal

Wake Island

MARSHALL ISLANDS

GILBERT ISLANDS

Battle of Tarawa

N

Battle of Midway

Midway

ALEUTIAN ISLANDS

Alaska (USA)

Japanese attack on Pearl Harbor

Oahu

HAWAIIAN ISLANDS

CHRONOLOGY OF WORLD WAR II IN THE PACIFIC

December 7, 1941	Japan attacks the U.S. naval base at Pearl Harbor.
December 8, 1941	The United States declares war on Japan. Japan bombs the Philippines.
December 1941– April 1942	Japan expands further across the Pacific with victories in the Philippines, Guam, Wake Island, the Dutch East Indies, Malaya, and the Solomon Islands.
April 9, 1942	U.S. troops surrender at Bataan in the Philippines.
May 7–8, 1942	The U.S. and Japanese navies fight the Battle of the Coral Sea.
June 4–6, 1942	The Japanese advance is stopped at the Battle of Midway.
August 7, 1942	U.S. Marines land on Guadalcanal in the Solomon Islands.
November 21, 1943	U.S. forces begin attacks on the Gilbert Islands.
January 31, 1944	U.S. forces begin attacks on the Marshall Islands.
July 21, 1944	U.S. forces begin attacks on Guam, in the Mariana Islands.
December 15, 1944	U.S. forces land in the Philippines.
February 19, 1945	U.S. forces land on Iwo Jima, Japan.
April 1, 1945	U.S. forces land on Okinawa, Japan.
August 6, 1945	The *Enola Gay* drops an atomic bomb on Hiroshima, Japan.
August 9, 1945	The *Bockscar* drops an atomic bomb on Nagasaki, Japan.
August 14, 1945	Japan surrenders.
September 2, 1945	Japan signs surrender documents aboard the USS *Missouri*.

Source Notes

6   John Bartlett, *Familiar Quotations*, 16th ed. (Boston: Little, Brown, 1992), 649.

10 Dan Van Der Vat, *Pearl Harbor: The Day of Infamy—An Illustrated History* (Toronto: Madison Press, 2001), 85.

15 Gordon W. Prange, *December 7, 1941: The Day the Japanese Attacked Pearl Harbor* (New York: McGraw-Hill, 1988), 118.

16 Walter Lord, *Day of Infamy* (New York: Holt, Rinehart and Winston, 1957), 98.

16–17 Robert S. LaForte and Ronald E. Marcello, eds., *Remembering Pearl Harbor* (Wilmington, DE: A Scholarly Resources Imprint, 1991), 19.

17 Editors of the Army Times, *Pearl Harbor and Hawaii* (New York: Walker, 1971), 72.

17 Lord, *Day of Infamy*, 98.

17 Prange, *December 7, 1941*, 129.

17 Van Der Vat, *Pearl Harbor*, 85.

17 Ibid.

17–18 Ibid.

18 Gordon W. Prange, *At Dawn We Slept* (New York: McGraw-Hill, 1981), 508.

19 Editors of the Army Times, *Pearl Harbor and Hawaii*, 72.

19 Lord, *Day of Infamy*, 124.

20 Harry Spiller, *Pearl Harbor Survivors: An Oral History of 24 Servicemen* (Jefferson, NC: McFarland, 2002), 24.

21 Bartlett, *Familiar Quotations*, 649.

22 Ronnie Day, ed., *Mack Morriss: South Pacific Diary 1942–43* (Lexington: University Press of Kentucky, 1996), 54–56.

22 Edwin T. Layton, *And I Was There* (New York: William Morrow, 1985), 354.

23–24 Henry Clausen and Bruce Lee, *Pearl Harbor: Final Judgment* (New York: Crown, 1992), 310.

24 Ibid.

25 Kerry L. Lane, *Guadalcanal Marine* (Jackson: University Press of Mississippi, 2004), 93.

26 Gene Boyt, *Bataan: A Survivor's Story* (Norman: University of Oklahoma Press, 2004), 121.

27 Day, *Mack Morriss*, 54–56.

28 George Lince, *Too Young the Heroes* (Jefferson, NC: McFarland, 1997), 58.

28 Paul D. Veatch, *Jungle, Sea and Occupation: A World War II Soldier's Memoir of the Pacific Theater* (Jefferson, NC: McFarland, 2000), 21.

32 Judith A. Bellafaire, "The Women's Army Corps: A Commemoration of World War II Services," U.S. Army Center of Military History, Publication 72–15, 7.

34 U.S. Army, "The Army Nurse Corps," U.S. Army Center of Military History, Publication 72–14, 5.

34 Ibid.

38 Alexander Molnar Jr., "Navajo Code Talkers," *Navy & Marine Corps World War II Commemorative Committee*, August 12, 1997, http://www.history.navy.mil/faqs/faq61-2.htm (September 12, 2006).

40 Homer H. Grantham, *Thunder in the Morning* (Fayetteville, AR: Phoenix International, 2003), 54.

40 Tim Brady, "Fighting Hunger," *History Channel Magazine*, (September–October 2005), 29.

41 Lane, *Guadalcanal Marine*, 185.

42 Herbert Christian Merillat, *Guadalcanal Remembered* (New York: Dodd, Mead, 1982), 123.

42 Lince, *Too Young*, 58.

43 Jane Weaver Poultron, ed. *A Better Legend: From the World War II Letters of Jack and Jane Poultron* (Charlottesville: University Press of Virginia, 1993), 126.

43 Merillat, *Guadalcanal Remembered*, 121.

43 Lince, *Too Young the Heroes*, 43.

43 Poultron, *A Better Legend*, 166.

44 Lane, *Guadalcanal Marine*, 75.

44 Ibid.

45 Floyd W. Radike, *Across the Dark Islands: The War in the Pacific* (New York: Ballantine, 2003), 134.

45 Lince, *Too Young the Heroes*, 45.

46 Department of the Navy, "Hermitage" *Dictionary of American Naval Fighting Ships* (Washington, DC: U.S. Department of the Navy, Naval Historical Center), n.d., http://www.history.navy.mil/danfs/h5/hermitage-i.htm (September 12, 2006).

47 Russell Davis, *Marine at War* (Boston: Little, Brown, 1961), 25.

48 John Hersey, *Into the Valley* (New York: Schocken, 1942), 46.

48 Patrick K. O'Donnell, *Into the Rising Sun: In Their Own Words, World War II's Pacific Veterans Reveal the Heart of Combat* (New York: Free Press, 2002), 83.

48–49 Robert Leckie, *Okinawa: The Last Battle of World War II* (New York: Viking Press, 1995), 99.

50 Richard Tregaskis, *Guadalcanal Diary* (New York: Random House, 1943), 148.

50 Ibid.

50 Abraham Felber, *The Old Breed of Marine* (Jefferson, NC: McFarland, 2003), 114.

50 Ibid.

50 Ibid.

50 Karal Ann Marling and John Wetenhall, *Iwo Jima* (Cambridge, MA: Harvard University Press, 1991), 97.

50 Parker Bishop Albee Jr. and Keller Cushing Freeman, *Shadows of Suribachi* (Westport, CT: Praeger, 1995), 26.

51 Ibid.

51 Ibid.

51 Ibid., 41.

52 Robert E. Allen, *The First Battalion of the 28th Marines on Iwo Jima* (Jefferson, NC: McFarland, 1999), 235.

52–53 Bill D. Ross, *Iwo Jima: Legacy of Valor* (New York: Vanguard Press, 1985), 316.

53 Merrill B. Twining, *No Bended Knee: The Battle for Guadalcanal* (Novato, CA: Presidio Press, 1996), 85.

54 Layton, *And I Was There*, 448.

56 Ibid.

56 Ibid.

57 Ibid.

57 James J. Fahey, *Pacific War Diary 1942–1945* (Boston: Houghton Mifflin, 1963), 37.

58 Ibid.

58 Bernard Ireland, *Jane's Naval History of World War II* (New York: Harper Collins, 1998), 95.

59 James F. Calvert, *Silent Running: My Years on a World War II Attack Submarine* (New York: John Wiley & Sons, 1995), 82.

59 Ibid.

59 Gerold Frank and James D. Horan, *U.S.S. Seawolf: Submarine Raider of the Pacific* (New York: G. P. Putnam's Sons, 1945), 92.

59–60 Gregory F. Michno, *U.S.S. Pampanito: Killer-Angel* (Norman: University of Oklahoma Press, 2000), 82, 86.

60 Edward L. Beach, *Submarine!* (New York: Holt, Rinehart and Winston, 1946), 70.

60 Ibid., 124.

61 Bobette Gugliotta, *Pigboat 39: An American Sub Goes to War* (Lexington: University Press of Kentucky, 1984), 153.

61 Ibid.

61 John A. Williamson, *Antisubmarine Warrior in the Pacific* (Tuscaloosa: University of Alabama Press, 2005), 116–117.

61 Ibid.

61 Ibid., 192.

61 C. Snelling Robinson, *200,000 Miles Aboard the Destroyer Cotton* (Kent, OH: Kent State University Press, 2000), 123.

62 Ibid., 147.

62 Ibid.

62 Ryuji Nagatsuka, *I Was a Kamikaze* (New York: Macmillan, 1972), 166.

62 Ibid., 197.

62 Albert Axell and Hideaki Kase, *Kamikaze: Japan's Suicide Gods* (London: Pearson Education, 2002), 3.

63 Ibid., 140.

63 Edwin P. Hoyt, *The Kamikazes* (New York: Arbor House, 1983), 139.

64 Quentin Reynolds, *70,000 to 1: The Story of Lieutenant Gordon Manuel* (New York: Random House, 1946), 137.

65 Tom Brokaw, *The Greatest Generation* (New York: Random House, 1998), 117.

66 Reynolds, *70,000 to 1*, 137.

66 Eric M. Bergerud, *Fire in the Sky: The Air War in the South Pacific* (Boulder, CO: Westview Press, 2000), 524.

67 Ibid., 500.

67 John Howard McEniry Jr., *A Marine Dive-Bomber Pilot at Guadalcanal* (Tuscaloosa: University of Alabama Press, 1987), 74–75.

71 Hermann Knell, *To Destroy a City: Strategic Bombing and Its Human Consequence in World War II* (Cambridge, MA: Da Capo Press, 2003), 264.

71 Ibid.

71 Walter J. Boyne, *Clash of Wings: Air Power in World War II* (New York: Simon & Schuster, 1994), 369.

71 Knell, *To Destroy a City*, 266.

71 *Stars and Stripes*, "Largest B-29 Fleet Hits Nagoya with Fire Bombs," Mid-Pacific edition, May 14, 1945, 3.

72 John M. Wright Jr. *Captured on Corregidor: Diary of an American P.O.W. in World War II* (Jefferson, NC: McFarland, 1988), 9.

72 Ibid.

72 Tom Bird, *American POWs of World War II: Forgotten Men Tell Their Stories* (Westport, CT: Praeger, 1992), 7.

72 Ibid.

73 Andrew D. Carson, *My Time in Hell: Memoir of an American Soldier Imprisoned by the Japanese in World War II* (Jefferson, NC: McFarland, 1997), 32.

75 Wright, *Captured on Corregidor*, 133.

76 Bird, *American POWs*, 4.

76 Preston John Hubbard, *Apocalypse Undone: My Survival of Japanese Imprisonment during World War II* (Nashville: Vanderbilt University Press, 1990), 88.

76 Herbert Zincke, *Mitsui Madhouse* (Jefferson, NC: McFarland, 2003), 80.

77 Ibid.

77 John Henry Poncio and Martin Young, *Girocho: A GI's Story of Bataan and Beyond* (Baton Rouge: Louisiana State University Press, 2003), 86.

77 Boyt, *Bataan*, 222–224.

77 Ibid.

77 Hubbard, *Apocalypse Undone*, 198.

77 Chet Cunningham, *Hell Wouldn't Stop: An Oral History of the Battle of Wake Island* (New York: Carroll & Graf, 2002), 188–189.

78 Carson, *My Time in Hell*, 66.

78 Ibid.

78 Poncio and Young, *Girocho*, 61.

78 Ibid.

81 *Stars and Stripes*, "Okinawa GIs Go Wild, Yell, Fire Machine Guns and Flares," Mid-Pacific edition, May 14, 1945, 2.

81 John Hersey, *Hiroshima* (New York: Alfred A. Knopf, 1946), 12.

83 Gar Alperovitz, *The Decision to Use the Atomic Bomb* (New York: Alfred A. Knopf, 1995), 327.

83 Boyne, *Clash of Wings*, 374.

83 Oscar E. Gilbert, *Marine Tank Battles in the Pacific* (Cambridge, MA: Da Capo Press, 2001), 320–321.

84 Ibid.

84 Douglas J. MacEachin, *The Final Months of the War with Japan: Signals Intelligence, U.S. Invasion Planning, and the A-Bomb Decision* (Washington, DC: Central Intelligence Agency, 1998), 9, 17.

84 Ibid.

85 Radike, *Across the Dark Islands*, 249.

85 Ibid.

85–86 Veatch, *Jungle, Sea and Occupation*, 107.

88 *Stars and Stripes*, "Okinawa GIs," May 14, 1945, 2.

88 "Return to Peleliu," *Dateline*, NBC, August 4, 1995.

88 Ibid.

90 Harry S. Truman, "Address Broadcast to the Armed Forces, April 17, 1945," *Truman Presidential Museum and Library*, http://trumanlibrary .org/calendar/viewpapers.php ?pid=8 (June 1, 2007)

93 Ibid.

93 Ibid.

96 George W. Bush, "Remarks of President George W. Bush, National World War II Memorial Dedication, May 29, 2004," http://www.wwiimemorial.com/d edication2/speeches/Dedication -Bush.htm (June 1, 2007)

96 Robert Dole, "Remarks of Senator Bob Dole, National WWII Memorial Dedication, May 29, 2004," http:// www.wwiimemorial .com/dedication2/speeches/ Dedication-Dole.htm (June 1, 2007)

Selected Bibliography

Albee, Parker Bishop, Jr., and Keller Cushing Freeman. *Shadows of Suribachi.* Westport, CT: Praeger, 1995.

Allen, Robert E. *The First Battalion of the 28th Marines on Iwo Jima.* Jefferson, NC: McFarland, 1999.

Alperovitz, Gar. *The Decision to Use the Atomic Bomb.* New York: Alfred A. Knopf, 1995.

Axell, Albert, and Hideaki Kase. *Kamikaze: Japan's Suicide Gods.* London: Pearson Education, 2002.

Beach, Edward L. *Submarine!* New York: Holt, Rinehart and Winston, 1946.

Bellafaire, Judith A. "The Women's Army Corps: A Commemoration of World War II Services." U.S. Army Center of Military History. Publication 72-15.

Bergerud, Eric M. *Fire in the Sky: The Air War in the South Pacific.* Boulder, CO: Westview Press, 2000.

Bird, Tom. *American POWs of World War II: Forgotten Men Tell Their Stories.* Westport, CT: Praeger, 1992.

Boyne, Walter J. *Clash of Wings: Air Power in World War II.* New York: Simon & Schuster, 1994.

Boyt, Gene. *Bataan: A Survivor's Story.* Norman: University of Oklahoma Press, 2004.

Brokaw, Tom. *The Greatest Generation.* New York: Random House, 1998.

Calvert, James F. *Silent Running: My Years on a World War II Attack Submarine.* New York: John Wiley & Sons, 1995.

Carson, Andrew D. *My Time in Hell: Memoir of an American Soldier Imprisoned by the Japanese in World War II.* Jefferson, NC: McFarland, 1997.

Clausen, Henry, and Bruce Lee. *Pearl Harbor: Final Judgment.* New York: Crown, 1992.

Cunningham, Chet. *Hell Wouldn't Stop: An Oral History of the Battle of Wake Island.* New York: Carroll & Graf, 2002.

Davis, Russell. *Marine at War.* Boston: Little, Brown, 1961.

Day, Ronnie, ed. *Mack Morriss: South Pacific Diary 1942–43.* Lexington: University Press of Kentucky, 1996.

Department of Navy. "Hermitage." *Dictionary of American Naval Fighting Ships.* Washington, DC: U.S. Department of the Navy. Naval Historical Center. n.d. http://www.history.navy.mil/danfs/h5/hermitage-i.htm (September 12, 2006).

Editors of the Army Times. *Pearl Harbor and Hawaii.* New York: Walker, 1971.

Fahey, James J. *Pacific War Diary 1942–1945.* Boston: Houghton Mifflin, 1963.

Felber, Abraham. *The Old Breed of Marine.* Jefferson, NC: McFarland, 2003.

Frank, Gerold, and James D. Horan. *U.S.S. Seawolf: Submarine Raider of the Pacific.* New York: G. P. Putnam's Sons, 1945.

Gilbert, Oscar E. *Marine Tank Battles in the Pacific.* Cambridge, MA: Da Capo Press, 2001.

Grantham, Homer H. *Thunder in the Morning.* Fayetteville, AR: Phoenix International, 2003.

Gugliotta, Bobette. *Pigboat 39: An American Sub Goes to War.* Lexington: University Press of Kentucky, 1984.

Hersey, John. *Hiroshima.* New York: Alfred A. Knopf, 1946.

——*Into the Valley.* New York: Schocken, 1942.

Holmes, W. J. *Double-Edged Secrets: U.S. Naval Intelligence Operations in the Pacific during World War II.* Annapolis, MD: Naval Institute Press, 1979.

Hoyt, Edwin P. *The Kamikazes.* New York: Arbor House, 1983.

Hubbard, Preston John. *Apocalypse Undone: My Survival of Japanese Imprisonment during World War II.* Nashville: Vanderbilt University Press, 1990.

Ireland, Bernard. *Jane's Naval History of World War II.* New York: Harper Collins, 1998.

Knell, Hermann. *To Destroy a City: Strategic Bombing and Its Human Consequence in World War II.* Cambridge, MA: Da Capo Press, 2003.

LaForte, Robert S., and Ronald E. Marcello, eds. *Remembering Pearl Harbor.* Wilmington, DE: A Scholarly Resources Imprint, 1991.

Lane, Kerry L. *Guadalcanal Marine.* Jackson: University Press of Mississippi, 2004.

Layton, Edwin T. *And I Was There.* New York: William Morrow, 1985.

Leckie, Robert. *Okinawa: The Last Battle of World War II.* New York: Viking Press, 1995.

Lince, George. *Too Young the Heroes.* Jefferson, NC: McFarland, 1997.

Lord, Walter. *Day of Infamy.* New York: Holt, Rinehart and Winston, 1957.

MacEachin, Douglas J. *The Final Months of the War with Japan: Signals Intelligence, U.S. Invasion Planning, and the A-Bomb Decision.* Washington, DC: Central Intelligence Agency, 1998.

Marling, Karal Ann, and John Wetenhall. *Iwo Jima.* Cambridge, MA: Harvard University Press, 1991.

McEniry, John Howard, Jr. *A Marine Dive-Bomber Pilot at Guadalcanal.* Tuscaloosa: University of Alabama Press, 1987.

Merillat, Herbert Christian. *Guadalcanal Remembered.* New York: Dodd, Mead, 1982.

Michno, Gregory F. *U.S.S. Pampanito: Killer-Angel.* Norman: University of Oklahoma Press, 2000.

Molnar, Alexander, Jr. "Navajo Code Talkers." *Navy & Marine Corps World War II Commemorative Committee.* August 12, 1997. http://www.history.navy.mil/faqs/faq61-2.htm (September 12, 2006)

O'Donnell, Patrick K. *Into the Rising Sun: In Their Own Words, World War II's Pacific Veterans Reveal the Heart of Combat.* New York: Free Press, 2002.

Poncio, John Henry, and Martin Young. *Girocho: A GI's Story of Bataan and Beyond.* Baton Rouge: Louisiana State University Press, 2003.

Poultron, Jane Weaver, ed. *A Better Legend: From the World War II Letters of Jack and Jane Poultron.* Charlottesville: University Press of Virginia, 1993.

Prange, Gordon W. *At Dawn We Slept.* New York: McGraw-Hill, 1981.

——*December 7, 1941: The Day the Japanese Attacked Pearl Harbor.* New York: McGraw-Hill, 1988.

Radike, Floyd W. *Across the Dark Islands: The War in the Pacific.* New York: Ballantine, 2003.

Reynolds, Quentin. *70,000 to 1: The Story of Lieutenant Gordon Manuel.* New York: Random House, 1946.

Robinson, C. Snelling. *200,000 Miles Aboard the Destroyer Cotton.* Kent, OH: Kent State University Press, 2000.

Ross, Bill D. *Iwo Jima: Legacy of Valor.* New York: Vanguard Press, 1985.

Ryuji Nagatsuka. *I Was a Kamikaze.* New York: Macmillan, 1972.

Spiller, Harry. *Pearl Harbor Survivors: An Oral History of 24 Servicemen.* Jefferson, NC: McFarland, 2002.

Stars and Stripes Mid-Pacific edition, May 14, 1945.

Taylor, Theodore. *Air Raid—Pearl Harbor.* New York: Thomas Y. Crowell, 1971.

Tregaskis, Richard. *Guadalcanal Diary.* New York: Random House, 1943.

Twining, Merrill B. *No Bended Knee: The Battle for Guadalcanal.* Novato, CA: Presidio Press, 1996.

U.S. Army. "The Army Nurse Corps." U.S. Army Center of Military History. Publication 72-14.

Van Der Vat, Dan. *Pearl Harbor: The Day of Infamy—An Illustrated History.* Toronto: Madison Press, 2001.

Veatch, Paul D. *Jungle, Sea and Occupation: A World War II Soldier's Memoir of the Pacific Theater.* Jefferson, NC: McFarland, 2000.

Williamson, John A. *Antisubmarine Warrior in the Pacific.* Tuscaloosa: University of Alabama Press, 2005.

Wright, John M., Jr. *Captured on Corregidor: Diary of an American P.O.W. in World War II.* Jefferson, NC: McFarland, 1988.

Zincke, Herbert. *Mitsui Madhouse.* Jefferson, NC: McFarland, 2003.

Further Information and Websites

Books

Aaseng, Nathan. *Navajo Code Talkers*. Madison, WI: Demco Media, 2002.

Adams, Simon. *Eyewitness: World War II*. New York: DK Publishing, 2000.

Ambrose, Stephen E. *The Good Fight: How World War II Was Won*. New York: Atheneum, 2001.

French, Michael. *Flags of Our Fathers: Heroes of Iwo Jima*. New York: Delacorte Books for Young Readers, 2003.

Humble, Richard. *A World War II Submarine*. New York: Peter Bedrick Books, 2001.

Landau, Elaine. *Suicide Bombers*. Minneapolis: Twenty-First Century Books, 2007.

Lawton, Clive. *Hiroshima*. Cambridge, MA: Candlewick Press, 2004.

Taylor, Theodore. *Air Raid—Pearl Harbor!: The Story of December 7, 1941*. New York: Gulliver Books, 2001.

Whitman, Sylvia. *Uncle Sam Wants You!* Minneapolis: Twenty-First Century Books, 1993.

Williams, Barbara. *World War II: Pacific*. Minneapolis: Twenty-First Century Books, 2005.

Wilmott, H. P. *Pearl Harbor*. London: Weidenfeld & Nicolson, 2003.

Websites

HyperWar: A Hypertext History of the Second World War
http://www.ibiblio.org/hyperwar
"World War II on the World Wide Web" is attempting to provide a complete collection of official documents of the U.S. government dealing with the war.

Library of Congress American Memory
http://memory.loc.gov/ammem
The Library of Congress American Memories collection includes photographs, documents, and audio clips documenting the United States in World War II.

Medal of Honor Citations
http://www.army.mil/cmh-pg/Moh1.htm
The United States Army Center for Military History maintains this site, which lists all persons ever awarded the Medal of Honor and what they did to earn it.

The National Archives
http://www.archives.gov
As with any topic in U.S. history, the National Archives provides digitized documents and/or photographs. Use http://search.nara.gov to access the collection.

Smithsonian Institution National Air and Space Museum
http://www.nasm.si.edu/research/aero/aircraft/boeing_b29.htm
The National Air and Space Museum has a collection of important planes from World War II, including the *Enola Gay*, featured in this link.

U.S. Naval Historical Center
http://www.history.navy.mil/index.html
The U.S. Naval Historical Center provides photographs and information on naval vessels from all eras of U.S. history.

USS *Arizona* National Memorial
http://www.nps.gov/usar
This is the official site for the USS *Arizona* National Memorial, with a history of the attack on Pearl Harbor, photographs, and links to related sites that contain primary materials about the attack.

USS *Missouri* Memorial
http://www.ussmissouri.com/WebCam_live.html
This site allows you to take a virtual tour of the ship. It is part of a site that details the history of the *Missouri*.

INDEX

ABOUT THE AUTHOR

Susan Provost Beller is the author of twenty history books for young readers. She writes from her home in Charlotte, Vermont, when she is not either traveling to see historic sites or visiting with her three children and five grandchildren. Her one wish is that someone would invent a time machine so she could go back and really see the past!

PHOTO ACKNOWLEDGMENTS

The images in this book are used with the permission of: © Bettmann/CORBIS, pp. 2, 19, 21, 39, 49, 51, 65, 73, 74, 76, 85, 87; © MPI/Hulton Archive/Getty Images, pp. 7, 12, 82; © U.S. Navy/Getty Images, p. 8; National Archives, pp. 11, 14, 26, 27, 30, 31, 33, 37, 41, 42, 43, 45, 46, 48, 58, 63, 67, 68, 69, 80, 83, 96; U.S. Navy, p. 13; © CORBIS, pp. 15, 47, 60; Franklin D. Roosevelt Library, p. 16; AP Photo, pp. 18, 89, 91; © Keystone/Hulton Archive/Getty Images, pp. 23, 62, 84; © J. R. Eyerman/Time & Life Pictures/Getty Images, p. 29; US Air Force, Courtesy National Air and Space Museum, Smithsonian Institution (SI 91-1471), p. 32; Library of Congress, p. 35 (LC-USZ62-106313), 86 (LC-USZ62-20353); AP Photo/USAAF, p. 36; © Lou Lowery/Hulton Archive/Getty Images, p. 52; U.S. Marines, p. 53; AP Photo/U.S. Navy, p. 55; U.S. Naval Historical Center, p. 56; © Hulton-Deutsch Collection/CORBIS, p. 66; AP Photo/Dave Davis, p. 70; National Archives Pacific Region, p. 79; © George Skadding/Time & Life Pictures/Getty Images, p. 92; George Bush Presidential Library, p. 94 (left); John F. Kennedy Library, p. 94 (right); © Scott Smith/CORBIS, p. 95. Map by © Laura Westlund/Independent Picture Service, backgrounds, p. 98.

Cover: © A. A. M. Van der Heyden/Independent Picture Service (statue), © Laura Westlund/Independent Picture Service (map).